ABOUT
THE AUTHOR

Diemme Black is an author of sexy romance fiction. She has been married to her husband for over a decade and is still madly in love. She is a very busy mom and couldn't be prouder of her kids. Diemme likes to travel to all different beach destinations, and loves the sun and the sand. She thoroughly enjoys reading other romance and erotica novels.

Other books by Diemme Black include:

Inked My Life (Book 1 of The Tattooed Heart Series), which was published in 2014

Strumming Me (Book 2 of the Rokk Me Hard Series), which was published in 2016

If you want more information on Diemme Black, including her published and upcoming books, please visit and follow her at:

https://twitter.com/diemmeblack
https://www.facebook.com/diemme.black
https://www.facebook.com/diemmeblackauthor
https://www.instagram.com/diemmeblack
http://amzn.to/2bxJyoz
http://bit.ly/goodreadsDB
http://www.diemmeblack.com

BY DIEMME BLACK

ISBN 978-1-941432-03-7

ROCKING ME

BOOK I OF THE *ROKK ME HARD™* SERIES

© Copyright 2015 Diemme Black Publishing LLC

Cover designed by Shanoff Formats. Visit Shanoff Formats at http://www.shanoffformats.com.

First Printing, 2015

Printed in the United States of America

To my soul mate. You rock me and always will.

TABLE
OF CONTENTS

Chapter One _ 1

Chapter Two _ 21

Chapter Three _ 39

Chapter Four _ 49

Chapter Five _ 59

Chapter Six _ 67

Chapter Seven _ 83

Chapter Eight _ 99

Chapter Nine _ 123

Chapter Ten _ 141

Chapter Eleven _ 157

Chapter Twelve _ 171

Chapter Thirteen _ _ _ _ _ _ _ _ _ _ _ _ _ _ _ _ _ _ _ 179

Chapter Fourteen _ _ _ _ _ _ _ _ _ _ _ _ _ _ _ _ _ _ 189

Chapter Fifteen _ 205

CHAPTER
ONE

Ali

How am I supposed to survive the whole night in these whore heels? Seriously, how am I going to keep from literally hitting the dance floor tonight?   I absolutely cannot have one drink or I will fall down and probably break my neck. I don't even know why I am here to begin with. I'm a second grade teacher. What am I doing at a Las Vegas Strip nightclub opening party?

Easy answer: I have no idea how to say no to my best friend Sarah. She is in public relations and this club opening is her baby. She has movie stars, models, rock stars, and just plain old beautiful people here. Oh, and she has me. I am used to wearing slacks and a button down shirt most days when I'm at work. I'm a jeans and t-shirt kind of girl when I have time off. But not tonight. Tonight Sarah dressed me. I am in a black mini dress that hugs my lively hips. I do have to admit, it fits my hourglass shape quite well. The dress dips in the front with a huge charm pin holding the front down to show the crazy cleavage that I have going on tonight. My shoulder-length dark brown hair is pulled back from my face and curled to ringlets on top of my head. Sarah is not only my best friend, but most importantly is a fabulous person who always looks out for me. She did a great job turning me into Cinderella, if only for tonight.

I don't know anyone here other than Sarah and she is busy with work. So I mostly stay off to the side, near the dance floor. I so want to dance and forget all of my cares and heartache. But I don't want to look like a fool dancing all by myself. Let's face it, I am not going to meet Mr. Right here in a crazy Las Vegas nightclub. Actually, I don't want Mr. Right. I want Mr. Naughty.

So here is my sad story. I'm thirty-two and have a great job as a second grade teacher at the most exclusive school on the west coast. I have a small but amazing group of friends, which thankfully replaces my crappy family back on the east coast. It's not that I don't meet guys or date. But once we start to get intimate, it all goes downhill. I'm not a prude, far from it. I just haven't been able to meet a guy that's normal, healthy, hard working, and what I need in the bedroom. The last part is mostly the problem. I'm not saying that I'm a complete BDSM person. But I want a man to be in control. In a good way of course.

Maybe I should have brought a date with me tonight. At least I'd have someone to talk to right now, and a warm body to go home with. I can't seem to get the relationship thing right. I'm not sure if it's because I want rough and steamy sex or because most guys that I do tend to date for a few weeks try to change me.

There was Trey. He was pretty vanilla in the sack, but cute and doable. But after a few weeks of seeing each other, I noticed he kept taking me to vegetarian restaurants, trying to make me lose weight. That was the end of him.

Then there was Terry. He loved to talk dirty while we were having sex, which was great for me. But he seemed to be talking to himself. "Yeah, Terry, give it to her, give it to her hard." That was a bit weird, and hard to go along with.

Now Brad was someone who lasted a while, over a year in fact. But again, vanilla sex. In fact, in the year we were together, I was never on top. And the one time I tried dirty talk during sex, he completely freaked out and said that the language was disgusting and I should just remain quiet during sex. I have no idea why I even saw him again, but I did, and for a while no less. I had to break it off when he started to tell me he couldn't stand that I constantly talked about work. I am a second grade teacher, and I love my job and my kids. How was I supposed to be in a relationship with a man who didn't want to share my life? I had to break it off then, and to say he took it badly is an understatement. He told me I was lucky that he felt sorry enough to be with me, and that when he slept with me he had to close his eyes and picture a thinner girl to be able to ejaculate. And yes, he couldn't say the word cum, he had to use ejaculate.

It's been like that for a while now. I am a single, spinster school teacher, minus the seven cats. But on the plus side, I do have a nightstand drawer filled with ropes, vibrators and toys. So I guess that puts me on another plane than most school teachers, right? Now all I need is a man who wants to play bad boy with me.

I have yet to find a man who can make me hot and bothered and still keep me that way in the sack. I want someone who is naturally like I am. Someone who likes to talk dirty to me and likes to hold my hands firmly over my head as he ravishes me and makes me cum until I'm screaming his name and my legs are shaking. I should just chalk this night up to a dud and go home and have some fun with my vibrator and Mr. Jace Wikks. Oh, Jace Wikks, lead singer for Blacking Out. That's what I've named my big blue vibrator. That way as I cum, I scream Jace's name.

Blacking Out is my favorite band, a kind of hard rock, alternative music. Not only is Jace the lead singer, but he also is the main writer of all their music. Jace is about five years older than my thirty-two years. He is tall, over six feet and slim. I usually don't want the heroine-skinny guys in my bed, since I am far from a waif myself. But he is a ripped slim. You could always see his ripped abs at his shows. He is always on stage shirtless. His hair is a very-close-to-the-scalp shaved dark brown. Usually he has his two lip piercings in, but I have seen pictures where they're out. Tattoos litter his arms, chest and back. Not just any tattoos. He has a Tibetan temple on his back. His chest has tons of different sizes, shapes and styles of tattoos. His arms are full of tattoos of his different lyrics. He is a perfect male specimen for me. I owe him my most amazing orgasms. No man has ever been able to give me the orgasms I've had all by myself with my dildo and my great fantasies of Jace.

That's it, I'm getting myself hot and bothered just thinking about Jace and my dildo. I'm going home. I make my way towards the front of the club, near the red carpet, to find Sarah so I can tell her I am heading home. Just as I am walking towards her, my ho heels get snagged in the carpet and down I go. Well I guess I'm more graceful than I thought because I don't hit the floor. Wait, how do I not hit the floor? I look up and see the most devilish smile I've ever seen in my life. A gorgeous guy, who looks wickedly like none other than Jace Wikks, is holding me in his arms.

"Don't worry, I've got you, baby," he says to me as he holds on to my arms and lifts me up to set me back down on my feet.

"Wow, thank you." I'm not sure if my tongue is hanging out of my mouth like a drooling dog, but I physically shake my head and try not to act like a moron. "Has anyone ever told you that you look just like Jace Wikks?" I ask him.

He gives me a small smile and laughs. "Yeah, my mom thinks I look just like him. Personally, I don't see it. I hope you're not heading towards the door 'cause you're leaving. I just found you," he says.

"Actually, I was going to head out. This is not my sort of thing," I answer.

"What is your sort of thing?" he asks with a smile.

"Not really the club thing. I'm just here 'cause this is my friend's opening and she asked me to come here for moral support. But I'd rather be at a movie or at The Strike. What about you? Is this something you usually do, go clubbing?" I ask.

"I love The Strike. It's one of my favorite places on The Strip. Maybe we should cut this place and head there. What do you say?" he asks with a very gorgeous smile.

Don't ask me why I would immediately leave with a guy I totally just met, but away I go. I do decide to take my own car and tell him I'll meet him there after I say goodnight to Sarah. He smiles, brings my hand to his lips, kisses my hand and tells me to not take too long and that he'll meet me there. Then he just turns around and makes his way back out of the club. I totally have to find Sarah, and fast. I catch a glimpse of her and wave, and she comes running towards me.

"I'm so sorry to do this to you, but I am totally bailing on you. I met someone and we're meeting at The Strike to go bowling. You aren't mad, are you?"

"No way! Where is he? Is he hot?"

"Yes, he's totally hot and looks just like Jace Wikks."

"That's awesome! Go on, I'll talk to you tomorrow. Call me if anything happens and this guy turns out to be a loser and I'll send Michael to The Strike to save you. Love you, have fun," Sarah says and is whisked away in the crowd.

I make my way to the parking lot and to my car as fast as I can without killing myself in my stupid shoes, and then head to the coolest bowling alley on The Strip, The Strike. The music is blasting when I get there and people are having a great time. I look up and down all the alleys but there is no guy. Holy Shit. I don't even know the guy's name. Wow, I really am a whore. I agreed to meet a guy I knew a mere matter of minutes and didn't even know his name. Come to think of it, he hadn't even asked me my name either. I guess if someone yells "hey you" I should look to see if it's for me.

That's when it hits me; this is probably a huge joke at my expense. That guy is totally gorgeous, and I'm me. He could have had any girl at the club. Why would he want to leave, as soon as he got there, and with me? Call this the worst night ever. I should just go back to my car, hit In-N-Out and scream myself raw with my vibrator. I'll just do one whole walk of The Strike, then I'm out of here.

I walk all the way to the end of the alleys, near the VIP curtained section, and don't see my mystery man. Then I feel someone behind me and I turn around. Coming from the VIP section is mystery man.

"All the lanes are filled and they have a party coming, so they offered the VIP section. Hope that's okay," he says, looking a bit shy.

"No, that's fine. I don't have a ton of cash on me, since I only thought I'd be at the club and everything there was free. Did they say how much it would be?"

"Problem solved. They offered it at a huge discount, and I already paid. So, no worries."

"But there is another problem," I respond. "I have no idea what your name is. I feel ridiculous that I even have to ask. Isn't that like the first thing people tell each other? Especially before they decide to meet each other somewhere?"

He takes my hand and shakes it. "I'm Ryan Freace. It's lovely to meet you, Miss?" he asks.

"Ali, Ali Danielli. It's nice to meet you too. So, shall we bowl?"

"Let's get this party started," he says. I go into the

VIP section and am blown away. There's a bar, just for us, and five lanes, all for us. There is a food table being brought in as well. Just as I am in awe of the totally over-the-top place, a young woman walks my way.

"Hi, I'm Anna and I'll be seeing to you tonight. Would you like to change into something more comfortable? We have jeans and bowling shirts, socks and shoes. Just let me know what sizes you need and I'll go grab everything for you Miss…"

"Thank you, Anna, this is Ms. Danielli. Ali, just pick whatever you want, it's all included in the bowling package. I'm gonna take a size large shirt and size twelve shoes. Ali?" Ryan asks.

"I'll take a large shirt too and a size twelve jeans if you have, and a size eight shoe. Thanks."

I am so embarrassed to have said I am a size twelve in front of Ryan. Here could possibly be my sex God and I already kill the evening by telling him I am fat, as if he doesn't already know by looking at me. Oh crap, here comes the insecurity. Why is this guy even here with me? He probably thinks I am so easy, that's why. After all, after a whole ten seconds of talking to him, here I am alone with him, in a curtained off area, with a guy totally out of my league. Yeah, he thought he'd give me pity sex tonight so he could get his rocks off.

"Ali, you okay? You look a little off.""

"Yeah, I was just thinking about something. Never mind. I'm just gonna slip into the bathroom to change. Be right out." I am seconds away from a full blown panic attack.

I take the clothes that Anna is holding for me and run to the bathroom. It is bigger than the master bathroom in my house. Wow, panic hitting. I grab my phone from my tiny purse and call Sarah. She amazingly picks up on the second ring.

"Do you need me to send Michael there?" is the first

thing she says to me. Not even a hello or how are you.

"No, you don't need to send Michael. I'm just having a panic attack. I don't know why this guy is here with me. He could have had any girl in all of Vegas. Why me? I know you love me so you're gonna say all this nice shit about what a great person I am and how sweet I am. But he doesn't know that. He must think I never go out and thinks I'm an easy score. But I'm not sleeping with him just because we have the VIP lanes here. Right?"

"Wow, you have the VIP lanes? That's pretty sweet. And I wasn't going to blow sunshine up your ass, Ali. You are beautiful. You just think that because you're not a walking ad for anorexia that guys don't find you attractive. And you know what? I think people can see how amazing you are just from looking at you. Now grow a pair of balls and go have fun. Maybe you do want to sleep with him by the end of the night, maybe not. It's your choice. Now, just for now, push that all to the back of your mind, have fun and knock him dead with your stellar bowling skills. I love you. Have fun and call if you need us."

She drops the call then. I look in the mirror. I just don't see it. I think I am okay looking, but nothing special. I don't think I am the type of girl who makes you look twice. Why was he here? Forget it, let's just pull it together and have fun. He is hot, he looks like Jace Wikks and he wants to be here with me. But let's see what we can do with this hair of mine, and let's change up the make-up to make it more fun.

I take an elastic from my purse, put my hair up into a high ponytail, and poof it a bit. Then I take my eyeliner and make more of a cat eye with it. I am good with make-up, but hair is my downfall. My hair is usually in a messy bun or ponytail. I add a different darker lipstick color to my lips. I shimmy on the jeans and shirt, and tie the top at my waist to make my boobs look even bigger.

Now, if I could just get my socks and bowling shoes on without incident, all would be good.

Ryan

She is the type of girl that you see, and turn back to look at again. Her hair is dark brown with red highlights. Her green eyes are haunting and her mouth is made for sin. I can already picture my teeth tugging on her bottom lip asking for entrance into her mouth. I can picture her doing a lot of naughty things with that mouth. I have never picked up a girl so quickly since the whole fame thing started. Usually, the girls are coming after me. But tonight I walked into the club at the same time as some celebrity actor, so no one was really looking at me as I breezed in. I'm not used to people not recognizing me. This is cool. Ali thinks I am just any guy.

When she wanted to help pay for the VIP lounge, I thought I'd burst out laughing. I have enough money to buy it one hundred times over. But she wanted to chip in. That is so refreshing. Most girls I sleep with want a car the next day. There is something different with this girl. She doesn't know who I am, so she isn't after something. Maybe I should make a definite effort to stay out of her pants. That is going to be hard considering she already has something going for her: she doesn't know who I really am. Let's face it, I don't even know who I really am anymore.

Then again, maybe her not recognizing me is her whole little act. Maybe she knows damn well who I am, and ran here to bang a rock star? Wasn't that just like all women, take what you want and what you can get from me? Fuck what I need, only think about themselves. Fuck it. I'm overthinking again.

I just want to have fun tonight, and here I am. I'm in one of my favorite places, with a kick-ass girl and she hasn't a clue who I am. At least I hope that part is true. So I can be whoever I want to be tonight. Maybe even figure out who that is tonight. Oh shit, she is walking out of the bathroom. If I thought she was killing me with that skimpy little dress on, I'm now blown away as I stare at her in tight-ass jeans and a cute bowling shirt. Not to mention she did something to her hair, sporting a little rock a billy thing. I am in fucking lust with this girl. Could it get any better?

She walks towards me, and when she sees the food, her eyes widen. Yes, a girl who is going to eat, I'm truly in love. Ali picks up a hot wing and without a word, licks, sucks and eats the lucky thing dry. Has she any idea what she is doing to me? Thank God my pants are so tight. Hopefully they are tight enough that she can't see my dick growing just watching her eat a wing.

"Who goes first?" she asks as she cleans her hands.

"Ladies always first," I say. Then I think how that is always the case with me. Make a girl get what she wants first so I can then get what I want. But that thought hits me smack in the face. Looking at Ali's tight ass in her jeans is going to be the death of me. But seeing that she could actually bowl? Wow, what a girl!

We both bowl and eat and laugh and talk, and it is the single best date I have ever had. Ali not knowing who I am is amazing. I talk to her about my favorite things, from music to movies to books. We have so much in common. As she and I are talking, I can see she is trying too hard to hide her yawns. She is tired. But I just don't want this night to end.

I look at my watch, 4 A.M. I have to let the night end. She looks like she is going to fall asleep on the couch at The Strike.

"I guess we should call it a night. I'm so sleepy,"

she says.

"Yeah, I guess it's late. Or early. I have a few more hours 'til my flight."

"Flight? Where are you going?" she asks.

"I live in LA. I came in for the night to see some friends, but they all bailed and, well, I don't have my return flight until 8. I'll just head to the airport early and have some coffee. But first, let me walk you to your car."

"Well, why don't you follow me to my place and we can have some coffee until you are ready to head to the airport? I'm having a really nice time, and just don't feel like letting it end yet," she says with a shy smile.

"That would be great. I have a car out front waiting for me. A black sedan. Are you okay to drive or do you want to just grab a ride with me?"

"I'll need my car for tomorrow. But you can ride with me and talk to me to keep me company. Your car can follow. Sound good?" she asks.

I call Raymond and tell him the deal. He gives me a "very good, sir" and as we pull out of the parking structure, he is waiting and following.

"So I know your favorite movie and book and what music and art you like, but the big piece of information you have omitted. What do you do for a living?" Ali asks.

Fuck me! Here we go, I have to lie. Okay, well not lie, but stretch and bend the truth.

"I'm a writer. But I can't tell you much more about it, because I write under a pseudonym. Unless you get me crazy drunk, which I am not, I can't divulge that information."

She laughs and accepts my answer. Man, she's awesome. It is a short fifteen-minute drive to her place, a small but pretty tan and cream colored ranch style house. We pull into the garage and then make our way into her house. I stop dead in my tracks. Right on the wall, across from the doorway that I am standing in, is a poster of Jace Wikks. What the hell do I do now? The garage door opens into a hallway that separates the kitchen and living room. The living room is large and open with an L-shaped sectional that is a dark mocha color. The walls are light cream. There are framed art posters everywhere. One wall, the focal point is painted a deep crimson. Hanging on that wall is an incredible nude painting of a woman with her head back resting on the back of the chair, and her whole body wound in black thick rope, BDSM style. It is amazingly erotic and then I see the eyes. The whole picture is in shades of black, white and grays. But then I look at the eyes. The eyes of the woman are a bright and vibrant green. This is Ali.

"I usually take it down when I know I'm going to have company, but you slipped in past me before I could get to it," she says, fidgeting from foot to foot, clearly uncomfortable at my looking at her painting.

"Why would you ever take it down? It's amazing," I say, never tearing my eyes from the painting.

"Thanks. My friend Sarah – she's the one who did the club opening tonight – her fiancé is an artist and wanted to try his hand at BDSM and needed a willing model. I told Sarah to do it, but she never wants to be a part of his work. She says it would be too intimate for her to see the painting sold. So when she asked me, and she said it was fine, I did it. Then I just had to have it. I'm not sure why. I think that I was kind of scared that some creepy guy would buy it and jerk off to it, and that freaked me out. I always hoped that one day I would find someone special and then I would give it to them."

"Did you pose for any more? Or just this one?" I ask.

"Um, I did a set of three pieces. This one I had to have and the other two sold the night Michael had his first showing."

I walk closer to the painting to see the painter's signature without stopping to ask her. I am worried that she won't want me to know the painter's name. It is the hottest picture I had ever seen. I am so into BDSM art, and can't believe I hadn't heard of Michael Mailtlin. I am going to have to find his work and have it in my house. I not only have to have a piece of his art, but I know I must have a piece of Ali.

"Do you want something to drink? Beer, wine, vodka, coffee?" Ali asks, trying to get me away from the painting I'm sure.

"Yeah, how about coffee, if that's okay with you?" I ask.

"Sure, follow me into the kitchen," she says and starts walking.

I follow her and watch the sway of her hips. She has the juiciest ass that I have ever seen in a pair of jeans. Now I have seen girls purposefully sway their hips to try and draw my attention, but this is different. I can tell that Ali is different. She is just naturally sexy. I don't think she even realizes just how sexy she is. What a rare quality to find in a woman these days. Most women I date – or should I say take out to get them home to fuck – try to be sex kittens. With Ali, she just oozes sex without even trying. God I want her. Here I go, getting hard again. No, no matter what, I am not sleeping with her tonight. I am having a great time and really like talking to her and hearing her opinion of things. I don't want to ruin this with sex. I like her. I genuinely like this woman. I can't fuck her when she doesn't even know who I am.

Ali

I cannot believe Ryan saw my picture. I feel like a whore. I personally know that my painting is art, but that doesn't mean that everyone who sees it knows it's art and not porn. What must Ryan think of me? I knew I should have put it in my bedroom. But it is truly beautiful. I wanted it lit the right way and portrayed as the art that it is. Enough worrying now - I'll worry when he's gone.

I make coffee and, lucky for Ryan, he takes it black just like me as I never have cream or sugar in my house. We sit on my sofa, looking across at each other, and talk. At one point I walk past him over to the stereo, and put on Blacking Out. I put on a CD I had made of their ballads and softer music. I turn the volume low so we can just have them in the background. As I am walking past Ryan, back to where I was sitting, he grabs my hand. I look down into his eyes. They are blazing. They aren't just brown eyes. There are flecks of gold in them and the gold looks to be burning right now. I am overwhelmed and enthralled.

"Sit closer to me," he says.

I do, putting my coffee mug down on the sofa table behind us. I sit right next to him. He puts his mug down too, never breaking eye contact with me. He brings his hand to my cheek and smoothly caresses it. I lick my lips without realizing what I am doing. Then he moves in closer and gently kisses my lips. It is sweet and so light. He pulls back and looks into my eyes. This time, I move in towards him and kiss him. A little harder this time. Then I pull back. This is the dance we do, making sure that we are both on the same page. The next time, we both move into each other at the same time. A soft gentle kiss, then Ryan adds more pressure to the kiss and moves his hand to my cheek again. I put my hand into his short hair and bring him in even closer. We both shift on the couch and wind up crashing our chests together. When my breasts hit his chest, he moans. The moan makes me bold and I work aggressively to try and open his mouth. I move my tongue, begging entrance which he quickly allows. Our tongues twirl, and soon I am sucking his one lip piercing, tugging on the round hoop. He moans into my mouth and then his hands are rubbing my back. I lean back from his chest hoping that he will go for my breasts.

He gets the message. He runs his hands up the front of my shirt and finds my nipples straining against my bra. They are actually painfully hard. I want release. But I also don't want to appear the slut. So I moan when he runs his fingers around the hard little mounds. Then he starts to use both hands to fully explore my large breasts. He is in a frenzy and so am I. He pulls back, with heavy, lust-ridden eyes, and I rip the bowling shirt over my head and throw it. Then I tug at his bowling shirt, but he flinches and shakes his head.

"No, not yet. First let me take care of you," he says. I am so disappointed. I want to feel skin on skin with him. But at the moment when I am about to protest, he takes off my bra and throws it to the floor. Then one hand encircles my right breast and his mouth is sucking my left one. He uses just the right amount of pressure. His sucking is long and hard, and then he nibbles on my nipple. Oh God, just the way I like it. We are in such an awkward position, and I pull back, looking at him.

"Do you want me to stop?" he asks, breathing heavily with his chest heaving.

"No I just want a better position," I say, also out of breath.

He takes me in his arms and brings me down onto his lap. I am straddling him, and I can feel his hardness against my jeans. Oh my. I feel like a teenager as I rock against his jeans. We are dry humping and it is getting me crazy. I miss this. Nowadays, there is no foreplay, only straight to the bedroom. I love feeling his hard dick push against my pulsating clit. We are both rocking and breathing so heavily, I think we're going to hyperventilate.

I lean back, pushing my breasts into his face, and he obliges me by sucking them and making me so hot I think I'm going to cum right then and there. When I think it can't get any better, he starts to reach for the zipper of my jeans, and I shake my head, giving him passage to touch me.

Moment killed as his phone starts to ring. We both grudgingly part as he says he has to take it. He yells into the phone and answers that he'll be right out and not to call again.

"I have to go. It's time for me to head to the airport. But I don't want to leave like this. Babe, I can feel you wet through your jeans. Just tell me, do you want to cum for me?" he asks as he looks into my eyes.

I barely know him, have no idea how he'll make me cum in a matter of seconds, but hell yes, I want release. I nod my head in response and bite my lip, feeling shy about wanting to cum with a stranger. I'm not a prude, but I usually have a three date rule. But all men I've had, and there have been quite a few, seemed so plain and into their own release. But not Ryan. He wants me to cum, and I can feel how hard he is.

He smiles that devilish smile he had given me in the club and then his mouth descends on mine. He fucks my mouth with his tongue. That's how it feels. He juts his tongue in and out. It is amazing and then I feel his hand against my swollen clit. He is touching me over my jeans, but even over the thick material I am so swollen with want that I can clearly feel him. He rubs hard and fast over and over, and I moan again and again. My release is so close.

"That's my girl. I know you're close. I can feel your heart beating so fast for it. You want to cum so badly. I'm the one who's going to make you cum. Say my name, baby," he says in his sexy voice.

"Ryan. Oh God, Ryan. It feels so good. I'm so close."

"Can I unzip you?" he asks. "I want you to feel more."

"Oh God yes," I pant.

Ryan unzips my jeans and we both push them to the floor. I am in nothing but my black lace bra and panties. I climb back onto him, facing him and straddling his straining cock. I can see his jeans bulging, and I want to free him. I guess he read my mind.

"Next time we can do that, baby. I only have a few more minutes and I need to feel you cum for me." He dips one of his hands over my pussy and instantly lets out a rough growl.

"You're so fucking wet. You're wet for me, just me. Tell me you're only this wet for me," he demands. I love the way he talks to me in our lust-filled frenzy. It is so different from how he spoke to me all gentlemanly and well-mannered before when we spoke of art or music.

"I'm only this wet for you. No one else has ever made me this wet before. Please, Ryan, please touch me and make me cum for you. I want you to see me cum before you leave. Watch what you do to me," I beg.

He smiles and touches me again. Every touch through my wet panties puts me closer and closer to the edge. I feel the warm burn start in my belly and go slowly up my legs and then shoot through me as I throw my head back and scream and cum.

When I am able to breathe again, I look at Ryan with his wicked smile. He is so proud of himself. He kisses me, hard and deep. A car horn breaks our kiss.

"Baby, you have no idea how I don't want to leave after I've just found you. But I have to catch the damn plane." I climb off his lap and quickly dress as he tries to adjust his hard dick.

"Are you busy next weekend? If I can make it back in town Friday night, will you go to dinner with me?"

"I am free and I'd love to go to dinner with you."

We both smile at each other. We quickly exchange numbers and I walk him to the front door. I watch as he climbs into the car and pulls out of sight.

I walk myself to my bedroom and strip naked and fall into bed. I need sleep. I have been up for a full twenty-four hours and just had an amazing orgasm. I am bone tired.

I think of Ryan and hope I will hear from him soon. I go over the events of the night. Was I too forward? Was I much of a slut? For the first time in my life, I don't really care. I want him, and I don't care if he thinks the worst of me because of it. I want to sleep, but every time I close my eyes, all I can see is Ryan's golden brown eyes looking back at me with that sexy smile.

I don't know how long it took for me to sleep, but I had one hell of a dream about Ryan when I did finally doze off.

Ryan

I know I spent only a few short hours with Ali, but watching her as she watches me pull away is really hard. I want to stay with her. I want to carry her to her bed and lick every inch of her body. I could tell by the little comments she made throughout the night that she didn't see herself as sexy or beautiful. I hope she doesn't think

I feel that way about her.

"Good night boss?" Raymond asks.

"I know you're going to think I'm drunk, but tonight, I met the woman that I'm going to marry."

Raymond lets out a low laugh. "I don't think you're drunk. I felt the same way the first time I looked at my wife. Ten years and three kids later, I still feel crazy ass in love with her. What's her name?" Raymond asks.

"Her name is Ali. She's a teacher and she's incredible. Only one problem. I didn't tell her who I am. I told her that I'm Ryan. Seriously, Raymond, I have never felt like this before. The only feeling that came close was when Matt's family took me in. I felt peace. I feel that with her. She doesn't just say what she thinks I want to hear. She has a job. She has a brain and she has opinions. She's like no one I've ever met before. Think she'll be alright about the little white lie?" I ask.

"Sir, you can't start a relationship with a lie," Raymond says and looks at me in the rearview mirror.

"I know. But it was so nice to have her like me for me. We had a real date and she actually ate in front of me, made me coffee and just acted like I was normal. I'll tell her the truth this weekend. I have a date to come back here for the weekend. That okay for you?" I ask Raymond.

"Where you go, I go. You're the boss."

I am silent the rest of the ride to McCarran Airport. The trip through security is thankfully uneventful and so is the flight. When I land there are a few paparazzi but nothing too crazy. I still haven't slept. I just want to be home in my bed where I can think of Ali alone without embarrassing myself with wood that everyone could see. I have never been so happy to be home. I climb the stairs to my bedroom and start to undress. I have the faint smell of Ali's perfume on me. I am still so horny for her. I can't help myself. I climb naked onto my bed and grab the bottle of lube from the nightstand and jerk off thinking of Ali.

CHAPTER
TWO

Ryan

The week is dragging by. We have scheduled studio time to practice. We don't yet have a tour set, thankfully. But we are going to do a little set at some big New Year's Eve party for celebrities and music people. The guys want to have a new song for that night. But I am dry. I need a break and I need a normal life for a while. I keep thinking about Ali. I have called her a few times, but I am purposely keeping them to a minimum, so I don't act like a teenage asshole. Truth is, I love talking to her. This is something that is new to me.

I was never a talker. I learned that from my parents. Be loud, ask the wrong question, give the wrong answer, get hit. It was better to just be quiet and as invisible as possible. I was never a big talker with the girls I had revolving through my bed. To be honest, even when I did try to have a conversation with any of them, they seemed completely brainless. They only talked about themselves, never asking how I felt about something or about my past. Considering I never gave interviews, you'd think they would want to know something about me. But no, they would talk about themselves. There were also the girls who had no opinion about anything at all.

I would ask them what they wanted to eat, and the answer I always got was, whatever you want to eat. What kind of movie should we watch? Whatever movie you want to watch. I hate that even more than I dislike girls who are only into themselves. I started to roll through girls, and even when I tried to have a relationship, I kept coming up empty. None of them could hold a candle to Ali. But then again, they knew who I was. Ali is still in the dark. But I am going to correct that this weekend.

I am at the studio, trying to write, but nothing is coming. Well, that's not exactly true. I am thinking of Ali, and there are words coming to mind, but love songs are not exactly our genre. I can't seem to translate into a song all the words I want to say, unless I want to be beat up by the band. I am close to trying to explain my problem to them. But then think about how it would probably go.

One, I know they'll just mock me. Two, I don't think that any of them, except for Alex, will understand.

Alex is the drummer for our band and he had been engaged to Cecelia. Things unfortunately did not work so well for them. But when they were together, they were inseparable. I remember Alex explaining it to me one night when I complained about love and about needing someone in my life who would listen to me and want to hear my true voice. He told me that the first time he saw Cecelia, he just knew. He said she was an obsession he didn't want to even get over.

That is what I am feeling now for Ali. I have been speaking to her every night since I got back to LA. I have heard all about her days at work and lied about mine. I have been telling her how I have writer's block, which is true, and that my boss is getting pissed about it, again the truth. But I haven't told her about the studio time, or the record label breathing down my back for another album. Truthfully, I think all the guys are actually happy for the break in schedule. Once we head back in to record, it won't be long until we are back on the road. Fun sure, but also hell.

By Thursday night, I begin feeling like I am going to

jump out of my skin waiting to see Ali. I decide that I can't wait any longer to see her. I hop an earlier flight and have Raymond take me to meet her at her school.

You would think they are guarding the President at this place. There are guards, none of whom wants to let me through since I hadn't told Ali I was coming to school. She is in class, so they won't call her to get approval. So I wait outside the school, at the gates like a sick puppy, waiting for the moment I can see her.

I hear the ringing of what I assume is the final bell, and as kids begin pouring out I pull my shades lower to my eyes and take the baseball hat that Raymond offered. I look like a pervert in my getup, but I don't want people to recognize me. There she is, my girl. That's what hits me when I see her running towards me. She makes her way past the kids and flings herself into my arms.

"The guards called and said you were here. But I was already getting the kids ready for dismissal. I'm sorry they wouldn't let you through. We have some celebrities' kids here, so security is super tight."

"No worries. I just really wanted to surprise you and see you," I say.

"Well, I am very happily surprised. Come with me so I can get my stuff. Then we can get out of here and start the weekend off right." Ali grabs my arm and drags me to her classroom. It is so cute. There are little tables and chairs. Her room is full of all different bright colors. You could tell how much she loves her job and how happy she is that I am seeing it. She is showing me all the projects that her kids are doing. We walk through the hall towards the door and I can't help but grab her hand. It just feels right.

We are walking out of the main lobby doors when someone behind us calls her name. We both turn around. I make sure to keep my head down and start to shuffle my feet.

"Ali, sorry to bother you when you're heading out for the weekend. Mrs. McGrath still isn't feeling well and doesn't think she'll be back for the beginning of the week. Would it be a problem if you took her class on the field trip with your class? I know it doubles the kids you're responsible for, but I would hate for them to miss out just because she's sick." The tall slender woman is ringing her hands as she speaks to Ali.

"Sure I'll take them. Does she already have parent chaperones, or should I call more from my class?" Ali asks.

"No, she has them all set. You just need to make sure they're all on the bus and behaving well at the science center. Thank you, Ali. I can always rely on you. Thank you so much. Have a great weekend." With that, the tall woman turns around and disappears around the corner.

"Sorry, I didn't get to introduce you to the headmaster. That's Mrs. Lenon. She's really great. You'll meet her another time. So are you ready to start the weekend?" Ali asks as she squeezes my hand more tightly. I kiss her softly on the cheek and whisper yes in her ear.

I drive with Ali in her car as we head to her house, and Raymond follows. When we get to her house, I just want to kick the door closed and ravish her in her bed. But not yet. Not when I have been giving her half-truths. I walk into the house with her. She kicks off her shoes and goes straight to get glasses of wine for both of us. We sit down on the couch together. I love this couch, her whole house really. It feels warm and homey and safe.

"So did you already make plans for where we're going to eat, or do you need me to recommend a place?" Ali asks.

"I don't usually spend too much time here. I'd like

to take you somewhere nice and quiet and private. Know where we should go?" I ask.

"I have the perfect place. It's a little pricey, but totally private. In fact, all the booths have curtains around them for privacy. It's French food. How does that sound?" Ali asks.

How precious is this girl? She is worried about the price of the meal. I could buy her a house right now with all the money I have, not to mention I have no spending limit on my credit cards. I tell her the French place sounds great. She says she wants to change and she runs to her room. It takes all my manners to stay there in the living room, as I think about the Jace Wikks poster. I walk as quietly as I can to the poster. It is signed. I examine the signature, and sure enough it is real. I wonder how much it set her back. I wonder why a woman who has beautiful artwork around her house would have this poster framed among fine art. Busted. I don't realize that I am staring at it so long - long enough for her to change and catch me at the poster.

"Is something wrong? Please don't say that you're not a Blacking Out fan. That could actually be a deal breaker for me," Ali warns, as I look like a cat that just ate the family pet fish.

"I was just wondering why you have this with all the real art you have hanging. It seems a little… out of place," I say.

"I know, it sometimes makes me feel like a prepubescent teen. A grown woman having a poster of a rock star. But fact is, I had been in a really bad place for a while when I was in college. I didn't know what I wanted to do, where I wanted to live. I just felt lost. My friend Sarah wanted to cheer me up, so she bought tickets to this show. This was when we both lived back in New York. Blacking Out, they weren't really known back then. But I went, hoping to just forget all my problems for the night. The moment Jace Wikks started to sing, and I really listened to his words, I felt calm. I felt like he was singing just to me. The whole audience, and stage, they all melted away. It was just him singing to me and telling me it would be okay and that I wasn't alone. He sang this one song, Hold On. It had exactly the words I needed to hear. That night saved me.

"In fact, that night changed a lot of things for me. I decided that I wanted to finish out my degree in Education and become a teacher. I wanted to get a job and get out of New York. Sarah wanted to be a PR person. Her parents had already moved here, but we had decided to remain in New York until we finished college. We both decided to move, and Las Vegas just seemed to work. I'm crazy close with her family and so is she, and this place was great for both of our jobs. I know it sounds crazy, but whenever there's a major decision to make in my life, I put on their music, listen to a few songs, and when I hear Jace's voice and the words, it all seems to make sense, and I make my choice.

"I was really lucky that when I came out here with my degree, they needed teachers like mad. So I took my certification test, passed and got a job at my very first interview. After my first paycheck, I went down to Caesar's Palace and saw this music store and they had the poster. Look at what Jace signed," Ali says.

I look closer, and there are the words, *Just Hold On, Yours Jace*.

I feel the ground actually move at that moment. Am I right? Are we meant to be? Hold On, the song about depression and not letting it win. Was Ali depressed when she heard the words? Did they truly save her? I am truly speechless.

"Ryan, are you okay?" Ali asks, looking very concerned. "Oh, does this bother you? I hope you don't think that I'm dating you because you look like Jace. I mean, I think Jace is hot and I think you're hot. But I know you're not him. I'm here with you, not him," she reassures, standing on her tip toes and kissing me.

She gives me the gentlest kiss and then looks into my eyes. I see the truth. She likes me. She likes to talk to me on the phone before she goes to sleep. She looks forward to texting me when she finishes her morning coffee. She enjoys telling me which kids are excelling in school and which need help. She likes to ask me if I am able to write yet and how much writing I am getting done. She asks me to send her pictures of my bedroom so she will know what it looks like while we are on the phone. She wants me, not Jace. I don't deserve this woman.

I take her into my arms and kiss the hell out of her. When she finally pulls back, her eyes are hooded with lust. "If we don't leave now, I'm not going to be able to be a gentleman." She laughs and we are out the door.

Ali

I do feel badly for suggesting LeRae. It is an incredible restaurant, with great food and so romantic. I want romance with Ryan. I haven't been able to stop thinking about him the whole week. I want tonight to be special and romantic and I want to fuck the shit out of him when dinner is over. When we talked during the week, he told me that he was going to get a hotel room on The Strip so that we could spend the whole weekend together. So no phone call from his scary looking chauffer about his plane leaving. Why does he have a driver? I guess since he doesn't know his way around, and this way we can safely drink and drive home. Home, where I wish we were right now, in my bed. Okay, horny, let's just get through dinner.

"Do you come here often?" Ryan asks me.

"Not really. Sarah and I do eat here whenever we

want to celebrate. Actually, I helped her fiancé propose to her here. I'm not too fond of her fiancé at the moment, but he was really nice back then. The food is great. I've had almost everything on the menu, as I bet you can tell, and it's all great," I say.

"What do you mean, 'as I bet you can tell'?" Ryan asks, looking slightly annoyed.

"Well, I'm not exactly a size 0," I say, hiding my face in the menu.

"Ali, look at me. I don't even know what you're talking about. I think your body is gorgeous. And besides, who the hell wants a stick for a girlfriend?"

Shut the front door, did he just say girlfriend? Am I this hot ass man's girlfriend? Okay, just let it slide, he didn't mean it. Say something witty and quick before he realizes what he said and retracts it.

"Thank you, that's sweet of you to say. Now, what are you having?" I ask, nervously scanning the menu.

"I think I'll start with the escargots, then the beef wellington with pommes frites and cream spinach. What about you?" I ask her, but notice that she is staring at me like I have grown a head. "Did I say something wrong?"

"No, it's just that those are my favorite things at this place. I mean every single thing that you just said is what I love the most here. I will have exactly what you're having. In fact, I'll just let you order for the both of us," Ali says and puts her menu down.

"Would you like to pick the wine?" I ask and hand her the wine menu.

"No, you go ahead. I'm sure you're just going to pick my favorite anyway," Ali laughs.

Turns out, I am right. Ryan does in fact order one of my favorite wines. He does let me try it first, and I love it. When the waiter arrives to take our order for the meal, he stuns me by ordering in French for us both.

While we wait for dinner to arrive, we talk about music. Ryan surprises me by telling me he is a huge Blacking Out fan. He also likes U2 and Bob Marley. I feel like I am living a dream come true. How can we have such similar tastes in everything?

When our appetizers arrive, Ryan and I are so wrapped up in our discussion of Bob Marley that we don't even realize they had been set on the table. I dig in to my snails, and moan from the garlicky, buttery goodness. After I eat all of mine, I dig into the bread basket and am dipping the bread into the left over butter with garlic when I stop short. Great, now I taste like a mouth full of garlic. This is going to ruin the rest of the night. But Ryan surprises me; he must have seen the wheels turning in my head and seen my thoughts. He takes my hand in his, and brings the garlic soaked bread to his mouth and bites the bread, and I look in awe as the butter drips down his lips and he sticks his tongue out to lick it up. Okay, so we'll both have garlic breath. Nicely done, Ryan.

Dinner is amazing. Not just the delicious food. The conversation with Ryan is so easy. We even have the same favorite book, *Crime and Punishment*. And I can honestly say I am myself around him. I didn't just eat a salad. I didn't change my opinion around him. We get into a very heated debate about the recent welfare cuts. Even though we don't agree at all, we listen to each other and I don't feel like backing down or acting dumb around him. I usually act as if I'm the bimbo and the guy is teaching me stuff. I like to have people like me, but with Ryan, it seems that he just likes me for me. Then it hits me: what if he finds out about the other parts of me, the sexual me? But then again, he was talking dirty to me, and seemed to like to give a little pain with his pleasure. What if I could have the sex I really craved? This could be my dream relationship. But what about…. my secret? What if he couldn't handle it? Do I tell him and risk losing this already, or just keep it hidden?

"Ali, you're thinking too hard. I can see the wheels turning. What's the matter? I thought we were okay with our welfare differences?"

"It's not that. I was just thinking that I am having so much fun with you, and I hate that you live in LA. Sorry, I didn't mean to get all down."

"I have an idea about tomorrow night. My driver Raymond told me that there's a drive-in movie theatre here in Vegas. Are you free?" he asks.

"That sounds great. I've always wanted to go to the drive in. I hear there's a double feature every night. But I'm only going on one condition. You have to let me pay for everything tomorrow night," I tell him, since he wouldn't let me put any money towards dinner which I knew was crazy expensive.

"Okay. But when you meet my parents, don't ever let them know I let you pay for something on a date. They'd kill me," he laughs.

"Ryan, I need to make a stop by the supermarket and then another stop before I go home, do you mind?"

"No worries. Just tell Raymond where to go and he's all yours."

I give the directions to Raymond to get us to the supermarket. I know that Mrs. McGrath hasn't been well lately and I am worried about her. I want to get her some staples so she will have one less thing to worry about over the weekend. I open the door of the car, expecting Ryan to come with me, but he tells me he has to make an important phone call and that Raymond will go with me and keep me company. I tell him I don't need anyone, but he insists. So Raymond gets the cart and follows me around the supermarket.

I pick up bread, milk, and orange juice. Then a bunch of fresh fruits and veggies, and some soup and lunch meat. I think that will be good for her. After I load my card with a few bags' worth of food, I go to the cashier. Raymond and I argue for a few minutes because he says that Ryan insisted that he should pay for my things. But since they aren't for me, I can't take his money. I tell Raymond that he either lets me pay or I am going to leave the bags here and he will be depriving a sickly old lady of fresh food. So he lets me pay.

When I get in the car, Ryan is playing with his phone but is not on a call.

"I hope that didn't take too long. I wanted to get some groceries for Mrs. McGrath. I hope you don't mind, but I'd like to bring them by her place now, so she isn't freaking about having to go out this weekend while she doesn't feel well. Is that alright?"

"You bought her groceries?" Ryan asks with a stunned look on his face.

"Yes, is there something wrong with that? She's in her eighties and doesn't have anyone. She hasn't been feeling well, so I wanted her to have some fresh food. Don't worry, I didn't let Raymond pay for her stuff, but he did try. That's sweet of you, but this is on me. After all, it's my friend. Plus you just paid for that crazy expensive dinner. We should have split that you know."

Again, Ryan just looks at me with a shocked face, not saying a word.

"Okay, you're silence is starting to freak me out. What's wrong with what I did?" I actually am getting pissed by the way he seems to think what I did was wrong.

"There's nothing at all wrong with what you did. Except for the part where I told Raymond to pay for everything. I think what you did was amazingly sweet and thoughtful. I just don't think I've ever met anyone who would think to do such a thing. That's why I'm stunned. I think you're pretty incredible." Ryan leans in and kisses my cheek. "Now tell Raymond where Mrs. McGrath lives so we can get this stuff to her and make sure she's okay."

Raymond is great at following my directions. I am surprised when Ryan offers to carry the packages in to Mrs. McGrath. I lead the way to her door. I ring it and wait a long time before ringing again, knowing that she is older and would have a hard time getting to the door. When she opens it, I become more worried about her. Her skin looks ghostly white and paper thin on her face. But as soon as she sees me, her lovely smile stops my worrying. She invites Ryan and me in. I tell her about the packages I have for her and we both follow her to the kitchen to help her put them away. She offers to make us tea, but we tell her we will come back another time, that it is getting late. I make sure to leave my cell phone number on a pad she has by her phone, in case she needs me, and I tell her to promise to call me day or night if she needs anything at all. Then she kisses Ryan's and my cheeks and thanks us for being so thoughtful.

Ryan looks a little bewildered in the car. I ask him if something is wrong.

"I actually do quite a bit for different charities. But mostly I just send money. I don't often help people like that. It felt good, even though it was really you who did everything. I just got to carry the bags and take credit."

"Stop. You came with me to the market and drove me there, and helped me put her things away. You did want to pay for her things too. You did a lot. More than most people."

"That was what I was just about to say to you. Thank you for letting me be a part of helping her. She's very sweet. I hope she'll be okay."

"Me too. She's taught me so much about teaching kids. They teach you the different methods of teaching in school, but the practical day to day stuff, that's what you can only learn from other teachers on the job. I didn't even know how to take the attendance properly until I met her. She's been such a gift to me. I want to help her any way that I can."

Ryan listens to me the rest of the car ride back to my house. Unfortunately for me, he just walks me to my door and gives me a very chaste kiss on the lips before saying his good night. I am so bummed. Why didn't he come in? Maybe I grossed him out with eating the garlic butter and bread. Maybe something I did last weekend turned him off. But if he was turned off, he never needed to call me again, much less call and text me every day. But something was definitely off.

I noticed when we were at the restaurant that some young teenager kept trying to look through our curtain. I didn't blame her, Ryan was totally hot. But it really made him uncomfortable. In fact, he outright moved his chair and pulled at the curtain at one point. Maybe it was me. Maybe he was embarrassed of me. I know I'm just a plain Jane. I'm nothing stunning. But if he was dating me for sex, he definitely didn't take it tonight.

Totally confused and feeling like shit, I decide to just try and sleep it off. Ryan is a bundle of contradictions. He called me all the time and texted me through the week. He talked to me every night before I went to sleep. He texted me every morning to have a great day at work. He flew here just to see me and have a dating weekend. But then he was uncomfortable with people seeing us together. And he even wants to see a movie at a drive-in, where people won't see us together. OMG! Is he married and I'm the other woman? It would make complete sense. He is so smoking hot. He has to be taken. I'm such an idiot. But wait, if he were married, where is his wife when he's on the phone with me? I need to shut down my brain and go to sleep.

Then I panic. Maybe he had seen underneath my black leather bracelet. I wear the same black leather bracelet on my left wrist every day. I only take it off to shower, or at night when I'm alone because of what's underneath. Maybe he saw it, and figured everything out, and was so disgusted with me that he had to leave. He was probably going to call tomorrow with some sort of excuse and go back to LA, never to been seen or heard from again. Oh well. What can I do? Sleep, that's what I can do.

Sleep is not my friend though. I keep running different scenarios through my mind as to why a hot and obviously successful guy like Ryan would want someone like me. I can feel my heart beginning to sink. I feel like I am starting to drown. That old feeling of insecurity and depression is coming. I want to push it away. But no matter what I try to see in the mirror to change my mind about my appearance, I always see the same thing: nothing. My meds and therapy have helped me so much. But they aren't a complete fix for my problems. I look at the clock, 3:00 A.M., and I can't take the panic and tears that are there, threatening. I get out of bed and take a Xanax to help get me over the hump of depression that is very seriously hovering over me right now.

I don't know if my high school problems really started my depression or if they were just the catalyst that opened the door to my depression. As I lie in bed, I can still picture it all so clearly as if it were yesterday.

I was a sophomore in high school, a very small and private high school in my little Long Island town. Everyone knew everyone. The whole high school had only 200 students in it. I was crazy in love with a senior, Mitch Everheart. He was the captain of the basketball team, wrote for the newspaper and was in drama club. Everyone knew him and wanted to be friends with him. He was the guy who started the party when he walked into a room.

I had told only my small group of friends about my

crush on him. But I didn't think it was any secret. I could never play the game well, and whenever he was near, my eyes were always fixated on him. I also was on the newspaper and one day, one very fateful day, we were the only two in the newspaper room together. All alone. He was leaning over my shoulder trying to read my review of his play. I could feel his hot breath on my neck as he moved my long hair aside. As I turned to look at him, he kissed me.

Granted it was not my first kiss, but it had been the best kiss I had had, until Ryan that is. We groped and kissed and talked and before long, we were going steady. It was my dream come true. I felt like a princess. Suddenly I was so popular and special and everyone knew me not just as Ali, sophomore, but Ali, Mitch's girlfriend. He would drive me to and from school every day. I was at all the best parties. I had a date every weekend. It was everything I had wanted and more. Mitch was great to talk to and was someone with whom I could share my thoughts, dreams and fears. Before long, prom arrived. Mitch won prom king, and when Karen Fripton, a girl I hated and who was always mean to me, won as prom queen, Mitch refused to dance with her and danced with me instead. When the prom was over, all the seniors headed to Mitch's parents' house in the Hamptons. Mitch and I partied with his small group of friends for a while; unfortunately, Karen Fripton was among the party goers. Then Mitch brought me to his room. I lost my virginity to him that night. We had talked about it, and I knew I loved him enough to want him to be my first. He was so gentle and patient. He kept asking me if I was okay and kept making sure he wasn't hurting me. After it was over, he held me tightly in his arms, and then said he'd be right back, that he was getting us each some water.

It wasn't long until I heard Mitch and his friends erupting in laughter. I heard shouting and high fives being delivered. I threw my dress on in no time and crept into the hallway to hear what all the fuss was about. That's when I heard Mitch with my own ears, "I win, I nailed a virgin on prom night. Pay up, Phil." Then I saw Phil Larkinson hand Mitch a wad of cash.

"So what are you going to do now, Mitch?" Phil asked.

"I'm gonna nail her a few more times tonight then dump her when we get back home."

I had tears already flowing down my face. I was nothing more than a bet, a joke. I made my way back into Mitch's room and picked up the phone. I called my best friend Sarah and told her everything as quickly as I could. Then I told her where I was. She got her brother out of bed and together they made the long three hour drive to get me. She told me to pretend to be asleep when Mitch came back into the room and just to wait for them.

I crawled into bed, all dressed so I could make my escape, and luckily for me it was truly a while until Mitch came back in the room. I pretended to be tired and he left me alone while he watched television.

The doorbell rang and rang and someone was pounding on the door around 2:00 A.M. Mitch jumped from the bed with me quickly on his heels to answer the door. He pulled it open and that's when Joseph's fist connected with Mitch's nose, thoroughly breaking it. Joseph grabbed me and carried me out to the car with Sarah waiting for me. She wrapped me in a blanket and sat in the backseat with me. I thanked Joseph over and over not only for punching Mitch, but for coming to get me. That's when Joseph mumbled that he always thought Mitch was an asshole and that he'd always be there for me, that I was like a sister to him.

I cried the whole way home. Luckily for me, I had the whole summer before I had to go back to school, so I wasn't very big news by the time I started my junior year. But I was broken after that night. I felt like a piece of trash. I started to act like a bit of a slut. I could care less about who I slept with or whether someone wanted to date me because they liked me or they just wanted to get laid. My reputation was shot and I could have cared less. Sarah was always sticking up for me, and trying to make me change my evil ways. But it was useless. Until college.

That was my chance to be away, where no one knew about Mitch, and no one knew of my slutty ways. I had a few boyfriends, but I made sure to have a few dates at least before giving it up. But there was always that doubt in my mind that they were only being nice to get into my pants. I just always assumed from that moment on, guys only liked me for one reason.

But the time I have been spending with Ryan feels different. Maybe he has just been trying to make me feel different so that I wouldn't resist when he wanted to sleep with me. But then again, I haven't exactly been putting up a fight – I practically attacked him when he was on the couch last time he was here.

CHAPTER
THREE

Ali

Morning comes too quickly with the Xanax having helped me sleep. Now I just have to find a way to distract myself while I wait for my date with Ryan, if there is going to be one. Sarah is busy with work, and my few other friends are all busy running errands that they couldn't during the week. I guess I'll do laundry and clean up. Maybe that is a good idea. What if Ryan wants to come back to my place after the movie? I have to have the place look nice.

My phone beeps that a text is coming in as I am making my bed.

> *Don't suppose you already miss me and feel like meeting me for lunch?*

It is Ryan. What do I do? I do miss him and want to spend time with him, but do I do myself any favors by acting so desperately and so easily at his beck and call? Hell yes, he's hot as sin.

> *Sure. Where do you want to meet?*

> *Do you know where the Arts Lofts are? There's a southern restaurant called Mama's that is*

amazing. One hour good?

Be there in an hour. See you.

Great. Just about forty minutes for me to get ready. I have to shave my legs again, wash my hair and put on a full face of make-up. Wait a minute. Who am I impressing here? I know he's a great guy, but if I want this to be something real, something more than sex, I have to show him me, the Ali who does not put on makeup on a Saturday afternoon. Not to mention that the depression is starting to sneak back into me, and I just don't think I can bring myself to get all prettified. I do shower and shave my legs and arms, just in case. Then I throw on a pair of black yoga pants and a white and gray tank top. Chucks are on my feet and my hair is back in a pony tail. It is second nature to put the bracelet on, then I am done. This is Ali. This is weekend Ali for lunch – he is either going to take her or leave her. But no matter what, I am being true to myself.

I have to keep reminding myself to breathe on the way down to the restaurant. Then I get there and see him, and he looks so good and so fuckable. I should have put on my face. What a fuck wit I am.

Ryan

God she looks incredible. She looks all relaxed and rosy cheeked. I wonder if it is okay to tell a woman that she appears so incredible without makeup on. Oh don't get me wrong. Ali looks like a goddess when she is painted up, hair all done wearing a tiny tight outfit. But this, this is pure natural Ali, and I am hard already just looking at her cute pony tail with one hot pink streak in her hair and her chucks on. A woman who can wear chucks and tight black pants, and a tank. What more do I need? My heart starts to kick up as she walks towards me. She blushes when she sees me look her up and down in an approving gaze.

"You look amazing," I say to her and kiss her cheek.

"I was going to say the same thing to you," Ali says and giggles. "I guess you could say we both have great taste in footwear."

I am wearing jeans, a grey long sleeve t-shirt and my black chucks. You would have thought we were either married or lived together and got dressed to complement each other. We look that in sync. We are quickly seated and I am so happy to see that Ali's appetite wasn't a fluke. I'll admit it, I eat like a horse, but I don't have a nine-to-five job, so I do work out like a crazy person too. It's all part of the job. Not only do I have to write well and make people happy, but it helps to look the part too. The cut and ripped man of steel does have its share of benefits. Ali and I work our way though our food with an easy bit of conversation. It is easy to talk to her. That's the problem. She is so easy to be around. If I tell her the truth, would that end?

The biggest problem is, I want her, I wanted her so fucking badly. But I would be a total prick if I took her before she really knows who I am. I have to tell her. But now I am so scared that if I tell her, she'll be so mad at me she'll leave. My brain keeps trying to step in to tell me that the longer I wait to tell her, it is only going to get worse. Tonight, after the movie. I'll tell her tonight.

After lunch, we walk through the art galleries that are right in the same huge warehouse building as the restaurant. I have on a baseball cap and keep my eyes down. She will definitely wonder what's going on if I wear my shades indoors, so that isn't going to work. I have to hope for the best.

Things with Ali are getting crazy for me. We like the same art and hate the same things. Ali and I see this one painting that we both love. It is $5,000.00, a drop in the bucket for me. But how would I explain buying it for Ali? I'll go back later or call them and get the painting. It is a beautiful cityscape of Las Vegas at night with all the lights blurring, giving the appearance that the city is moving fast. Ali says it reminds her of how we met and clicked so quickly and how that would only happen in Vegas. I am thinking the same thing. Like a flash of lights, I am crazy for this woman. I just want to be with her all the time. I feel like I am breathing better with her around. Seeing the smile on her face when she says it reminds her of us, that makes my heart do a flip. I almost feel it stop for a brief moment.

The rest of the day we spend at Ali's house. I ask her what she would be doing if I hadn't barged into her house and her Saturday. She tells me she would have been doing laundry. So I tell her that I'll help if she shows me how to do it. She laughs at that, not realizing that I honestly haven't a clue as to how to do one's laundry. I tell her that in college, I had my many girlfriends do it, and that nowadays I just send everything out. Who would think that even doing laundry with a woman would be fun? As we wait for the laundry, we watch episodes from American Horror Story Asylum. This woman is great. We even love the same shows. We are curled on the couch together. The need to reach for her and touch her starts to overwhelm me. But I know I can't go there until I tell her the truth.

I settle for holding her hand and holding her head to my chest when she gets freaked out. I feel like a teenage boy. I am excited to simply hold Ali's hand. I am excited to be protecting her when she is scared. How am I going to protect her from my life? How am I supposed to protect her from who I am? I don't know if you would call it depression. But there have been moments in my life when things just haven't felt like they clicked.

When I have those moments, I go back to being the scared little kid who wouldn't talk. Before I can think about it too much, I am folding sheets and pillowcases with Ali. Then it is getting late and we are heading for the drive-in. We take Ali's car and I tell Raymond to hold back and make sure that she doesn't see him or the car. He is only there in case there is an emergency.

We back Ali's small SUV in so that we can open the trunk and watch from there. Ali packed blankets and pillows in the back of the car. Then she leaves me there in the car so that she can go get the popcorn and sodas. I don't want her to go by herself, but she refuses to let me go with her, saying that I will try and pay and this is on her. She even paid for the movie tickets. Even though I hate it, and know I could buy the whole theatre, it is nice to have a woman I know isn't seeing me for my money or connections. I miss her the whole ten minutes that she is gone, but once she is back we are cuddled beneath the blankets. Oh the things I want to do to her body while she is under this blanket. No one would even see or know. I would be able to make her shake with lust. But not yet. Not here. Maybe when I take her home.

The movie seems to take forever. There is no way this piece of crap movie is only an hour and a half. I want to put the moves on her while we are at the drive-in, but luck is so not on my side. The car to our left has a mom with a bunch of kids and the kids are actually sitting on folding chairs right in front of us. Then there is a car full of teens to our right. They keep trying to look into the car to see me. So I just get through the hell that is the movie and have kinky thoughts about Ali the whole time. The drive home, we are both very quiet. I think we are both thinking of the same thing, how we are going to jump one another as soon as the garage door shuts.

Was I right!

Ali

Call me a ho, or slut, or whatever you want. I am on my man like white on rice as soon as the door to the garage shuts. I push him into the wall, almost knocking my Jace Wikks poster to the floor. His mouth commands mine. He is gentle and hard at the same time. His lips are soft and fit perfectly to mine. But his tongue pushes so hard towards mine. Our tongues twirl and soon our hands are everywhere. I can't tell if I am pulling at my shirt, or he is. But soon it is on the floor. When I reach for his shirt, he puts his hands on mine and stops me.

"Ryan, I want to feel your chest against mine. I want skin on skin with you. Why do you keep stopping me?" I purr and almost cry at the same time. I don't remember ever physically wanting someone so badly before in my whole life.

He pulls me close to his chest and kisses the top of my head. "Ali, I have these… scars. And I'm a bit shy when it comes to them. Can we turn the lights off, that way you don't have to look at them? Then you can strip me as much as I want you to," Ryan says in between ragged breathes.

I guess I have been wrong about his seeing beneath my bracelet. He would have brought it up if he had, since he too has scars. I take his hand and walk him to the couch. It is becoming our little love nest, the couch. I sit him down, and look into this eyes.

"Scars don't bother me. I like you, all of you, scars or no scars. Now why don't we just get back to where we were and get that shirt to hit the floor and join mine."

"Baby, please. I know you don't care. But it still bothers me. Can we please just shut the lights?"

I stand up without another word and go to the lights,

turn them off and head back to the couch with Ryan. I slip off my bra. I can very slightly see him taking off his shirt in the darkness.

"Baby, sit on my lap," Ryan says in a very raw and throaty voice. It almost sounds pained.

I do as he commands, enjoying every feeling. That first hit, my hot skin against his, is like fireworks. I can feel my eyes tearing. It is an amazing feeling. It feels so hot and explosive. God, what is sex with this man going to feel like? I want to know so badly. But before we get there, we are working each other into quite a frenzy. We are dry humping each other, rocking back and forth, our mouths mating like we can't live without each other.

"Baby, tell me what you want. Is this enough or do you want more?" Ryan drags his mouth from mine to speak.

"More, I want more, Ryan."

"No, that's not good enough. You have to tell me what you want me to do. I want to hear you say exactly what you want me to do to you."

"Ryan, please. You know what I want."

"Baby, tell me. You know you want to say the words."

"Ryan, touch me. Strip off my pants and touch me. I'm wet for you," I say. I know it isn't enough and I'm not shy about what I want to say. I just don't know how he really feels. Does he really want to hear the words I want to say, or is that enough and he isn't really into dirty talk?

"Come on, Ali. I know you can do better than that. Now listen to me carefully. I know you are a hot as sin woman who knows exactly what she wants. I promise, baby, I'll give it all to you, but you have to open your mouth, your mouth that I want to fuck with my cock so badly, and fucking tell me what you want."

Fine, here goes nothing, and everything. "Ryan, baby, I want you down on your knees, pulling my pants off. Then I want you to hump me against my panties until they're dripping wet for you. Then push my panties aside and fuck me with your hand. Fuck me like it's your cock and make me cum 'til it's dripping down your hand. How's that for now?"

I sit back to look at him. I can barely see his eyes, but I do see that he appears to have stopped moving and is in shock. Hopefully it is a 'yeah this woman rocks' shock.

"I knew this was going to be great with you. That's exactly what I wanted to hear." Ryan pulls me off his lap and sets me gently down on the couch. I lift my butt in the air as he shimmies my pants down while on his knees. Then he sits down next to me on the couch and I reapply myself onto his lap. We both rock into each other. Now that I have on only a pair of silk panties, the feelings I am getting from his very hard dick straining against his jeans are driving me mad.

I am moaning so loudly, I don't know how I am not deafening Ryan. Then it only gets worse. Ryan moves my panties aside and two fingers slowly glide into my hot pussy. My whole body shudders at the feel of him inside of me. What is his dick going to feel like? It feels huge against his jeans. I need to know. But for now, I am riding my own wave of pleasure. I am so close, so very close. Then he is using his thumb against my clit. That is all it takes. A few small circles against my clit and the way he is rubbing my vaginal walls and I am done. I cry out Ryan's name and shudder and sag against him.

"Oh God, baby, do you feel how you came?" Ryan whispers into my ear. I feel between his jeans and my panties, and they are absolutely soaked. I know I have this thing where if I get myself off really good, thinking of Jace Wikks, I can cum in bucket loads. But I haven't ever done it with a guy, not this way. I am so embarrassed.

"Ryan, I'm so sorry. Here, give me your pants. I'll throw them in the wash and have them back to you in no time." I am climbing off him and thanking the Lord that Ryan wanted the lights off. I can feel tears coming down my cheeks. I guess my voice failed me as I scrambled off his lap, because he starts pulling me right back down to him.

"Ali, that was seriously the hottest thing I have ever had happen to me. To be able to make you cum like that, please don't be upset about it. I think it is hot as hell. Just as hot as you are." Ryan quiets my protests by kissing me. I know he can't be too disgusted by me, or he wouldn't be kissing me. I feel so much better when Ryan is kissing me. I feel like nothing from the outside world can hurt me.

I pull back a bit and put my arms around his neck and start to kiss his neck. I trail my tongue up and down is neck and feel his pulse picking up.

"Ali, I think I should go," Ryan says in a strained voice.

I whip my head back, and try with all my might to see his eyes. He just said I was hot, and I was kissing him, and I could tell he was still seriously hard as hell, so what is the problem?

"Did I do something wrong?" I ask with a shaking voice.

"Oh, baby, no. It's just that I don't think we should sleep together yet. There are things that I want you to know and I just can't yet. That's the only reason. I just want to pick you up in my arms and carry you to bed and have my way with you."

"What about just sleeping with me? Could you do that? I mean, just sleep. I know it must be hard and expensive for you to keep flying here and getting a room and taking me out. I don't know when we'll see each other again, and I don't want you to go yet. What if we just snuggle in bed and watch a movie or something and you stay over?" I ask, so very hopeful he will stay.

"I definitely would love to do that. Go on, I'll be right behind you," Ryan says.

I walk down the hall to my bedroom, just happy that I will have Ryan with me some more time. I feel that this dream of being with Ryan can end at any moment. He will wake up and realize that he is dating below himself and then where will I be? I am so scared. I know there is still so much more that we need to learn about each other, but what I know so far I like. I mean really, really like.

CHAPTER
FOUR

Ryan

Now would be the perfect time to just tell her. Why am I so scared to tell her who I am? She seems to like me. Why am I so scared that she might change her mind when she finds out who I really am? I guess because it makes me a lying bastard. Or maybe it would change her, maybe that's what I'm scared of. What if she turns into the wanting, snotty bitches I always seem to get tangled in? A whole night sleeping next to her – that is what I want so badly. Would I be able to really keep my hands to myself? Then again, I don't have to keep my hands to myself; I just have to keep her hands off me. I can still drive her crazy and in turn drive myself crazy.

I throw my shirt back on and head down the hallway towards Ali's room. She is in the bathroom with the door slightly ajar. I can see her changing. I might be a creep, but she did leave the door open a bit, so maybe she wants me to watch. I see her pull her shirt over her head, freeing her huge breasts with a thud, and a moan escapes her lips. It must suck to have to latch up those big bad boys. Then she kicks off her wet panties and pulls on a pair of short gray sweat pants and a white tank top. She quickly does this magical thing where she raises her hair on top of her head with little bits sweeping down over her cheeks. She looks like a goddess. How does she do it, and so quickly? She turns towards the door to exit and catches me looking at her. She smiles.

"Like what you see, Ryan?" she asks and does a little twirl. Then she goes to her closet and pulls out an old and large pair of black sweat pants. "These should fit you if you want something dry to put on. But if you want to sleep in my wetness, that's fine too," she says with a smile.

I grab the pants and just drop my jeans where I am standing. The bulge in my boxer briefs is very evident. I keep my eyes on Ali as she has her eyes on my body, looking like she is going to combust on the spot as she watches me undress and then put the sweats on. I slowly walk over to her and pull her into my arms. "Ali, you're awesome. Thanks for understanding me and for not pushing me. I know it seems weird, not taking my shirt off, but I just…" She cuts me off.

"Just wait one second. I know we haven't known each other a very long time, but if you want this to be anything real, you better learn real quickly, I say what I feel. And right now, what I feel like saying is, shut up. You have nothing to feel bad about. If you have scars and you don't want me to see them, and you don't want to talk about it, I respect that, and I'll respect your privacy. For now that is. There has to come a time, if this thing with us keeps going, that you're going to have to tell me the truth about what happened. I'll wait until you're ready, but please don't make that be forever. I want you to trust me and have faith in me that it honestly doesn't matter. I like you, Ryan, a lot. I'm not saying that to scare you or make you run, but, like I say, I say what I feel. Now, enough of that, no more sadness, let's just get in bed and watch a movie." With that, she takes my hand and brings me to bed with her. I have been thinking of all the sexual things I wanted to do to her in bed. Now I just want to hold her and watch a movie.

Something about the way she just accepts me has me feeling great and also like a shit. Maybe this is the time to tell her? Why am I being such a pussy about this? Because I am falling in love with her and am scared that she isn't there yet. If she isn't in love with me yet, there is still a chance I could lose her.

So I have to wait. Wait, and romance the shit out of her.

Ali

Ryan and I watch one of our mutual favorite movies, *The Spy Who Loved Me*. Turns out we are both James Bond fans. We watch the movie in each other's arms and easily fall asleep. I wake, with us tangled in each other. I can't tell whose legs or arms are whose. We are completely wrapped around each other. I can tell from Ryan's easy steady breaths that he is still asleep. I just watch him. I am falling in love with him. How could I not be? He is amazingly gorgeous, sweet, thoughtful and funny, and we have so much in common. But there are also downfalls to our relationship. We live in two different cities, and he is way out of my league. It won't be long until the sex isn't enough to hold him to me. I am overweight, and just ordinary looking. I can't understand why he is even here. Now I start to panic – am I so fat and ugly that he doesn't want to sleep with me? Are there really any scars, or is that just something he's saying to get me to back off?

Here we go with my low self-esteem again. Why can't I ever just be happy? Definitely something to talk to my shrink about this week. But look at him, so peaceful. So beautiful. Why is he here? Would he come all the way back to Vegas next weekend, just to see me? Am I worth the time and money? I also feel like a turd for keeping my mouth closed about my scars while he was telling me about his. I told him to trust me and eventually trust me enough to tell me, but I'm not even making any grand gesture to tell him.

Just then Ryan opens his eyes and a smile flashes across his face.

"Ali, stop the deep thoughts. You'll get wrinkles," he says in a sleepy voice.

"Who said I was deep in thought? I was just looking at an incredibly hot guy who for some reason is in my bed," I say with a smile that I know must look completely fake.

"Stop putting yourself down. Ali, I'm the one who doesn't deserve to be here with you. I have so much baggage, so much shit I have yet to tell you, and you just accept it all, and accept me. You're the amazing one. And I find you incredibly sexy and gorgeous," Ryan says and wraps me closer to himself. That is how we fall back asleep.

As I awake, I can tell that someone is looking at me. I smile and open my eyes to see Ryan looking at me with concern.

"What's the matter?" I ask him and snuggle closer to try and become part of his chest.

"I just wish I could tell you more, Ali. It's not that I don't want to. It's just that there's so much to tell. Most of it not exactly good. That's why I want to wait for us to have sex."

"So you're waiting until you feel comfortable to tell me about your past?" I am leaning on my arm to look him in the eyes.

"Yes. What did you think?" he asks, amused and laughing. "You can't think that I don't want to fuck the hell out of you!" But I guess my silence hit him. He suddenly stops laughing and looks at me with fire in his eyes. "You seriously can't see how much I want you, Ali?"

"I know it's probably a horrible trait in a woman, but I will just be honest with you. I have very low self-esteem, Ryan. I have stuff in my past too, stuff that led to the way I feel about myself. When I can, I will explain it all to you. But just like you want to keep your scars hidden, I have stuff I can't tell you yet either. So, when we get all hot and heavy and you just stop, I think it's because you're having second thoughts about me, or you just don't feel like you want me."

"I seriously don't know what to say to that, Ali. I totally want you; no, that's not right. I totally NEED you. I am crazy about you already. I just don't want us to be together and then I tell you about the past, and you feel betrayed. I want you to know what you're getting into. Just give me a little more time, okay? I want this to work between us. I just need to find the right time." Ryan is running his hand over his eyes.

"Okay. Enough heavy talk. What about some French toast and bacon for breakfast?" I ask getting out of bed and stretching in front of Ryan.

"Show me the way, baby," Ryan says and takes my hand leading us to the kitchen.

Ryan and I have breakfast together and then Raymond is at my door waiting to take Ryan to the airport. I hate these moments. I hate saying good-bye to him. I never know if he'll come back. But we hug and kiss and he is gone.

I get a text from him not two minutes later.

I already miss you. I hope you're missing me. Can I see you next weekend? I'll come to Vegas if you have time for me.

I miss you too. Of course I have time for you, always. What do you want to do?

How about a lazy around-the-house weekend?

Only on one condition.   Will you stay with me the whole weekend? No hotel.

It is the least I could do since he was always spending money on Raymond and a car and an airline ticket. His answer is pretty immediate.

You want me to stay at your house?

Yes, what do you say?

Sounds good to me.   But we have to talk about stuff when I get there and then you decide if you still want me to stay.

I thought we went through this.   You're not a criminal or married are you?

LOL!!   No to both.   I just want the weekend to work out. Have stuff to confess.

I'll listen. See you soon. Have a safe flight.

The week goes by so slowly.   Even though I am busy at work, I know it is because I am so scared about what Ryan has to tell me. What could he possibly have to tell me that has him so worried, so scared that I won't want him to stay with me? These thoughts plague me all week long.   We speak on the phone every night and I have been begging Ryan to talk to me before he gets here but he won't. He says that he wants to talk to me in person and tell me about things in his life. I am miserable most of the week.

I am so happy when Friday arrives and I am free from work, knowing Ryan is on his way. I order sushi for us and pick it up on my way home from school. I also stop and buy a bottle of wine for us. I shower and change into jeans and a tank top and have dinner spread out on the living room table when the doorbell rings.

I literally run to the door, and when I open it and see Ryan with a weekend bag in his hand, I launch myself into his arms. In the space of about a month, I have fallen in love. Of course I won't say the words; I don't want to scare him away. I am also terrified because the last time I told a guy that I loved him, I turned out to be a joke and bet for him to win.

Ryan holds me so close to him as I hold him. I wish he would open up to me, but I still want to give him time and not push him too quickly. After all, I haven't told him about what Mitch had done to me, and hypocrite I am not.

"Baby, I've missed you so much. I know it's only been five days, but this is getting where five days is too long not to see you. Maybe you should take a little vacation and come see me in LA for a while. We could have everyday together and, of course, every night," Ryan whispers in my ear, giving me chills.

"I can't just take a vacation. I have work. Maybe I can come out around Thanksgiving break. I normally just stay in town with Sarah. Her parents have kind of adopted me into their family. We just have a small family thing and then go Christmas shopping on Black Friday. I could spend Thanksgiving here with them and then head to you for the long weekend. That is unless you do a big family thing?" I inquire.

"I don't have any family anymore. My best friend,

Matt, I usually go to his parents' place for Thanksgiving. I guess you can say that they've adopted me into their family as well. But then I could be all yours."

"Then let's set it up."

"I get to pay for the ticket though. Do you want to stay with me, or would you be more comfortable staying at a hotel near me?" Ryan asks, as he finally puts me down and walks me to the couch.

He kicks off his shoes, throws his bag on the floor and brings me down to the couch with him.

"I don't know how much work you'll have. Is it easier to have me at a hotel?" I ask, secretly hoping that Ryan is going to ask me to stay with him, but he is the one who mentioned a hotel.

"Baby, I'd rather have you to myself in my bed. Stay with me, if you're okay with that. I would rather you stayed with me."

"Then it's settled. I'll fly to you on Friday and we can hit the malls to go shopping. Then the rest of the weekend, we can just veg out at your place. Sound good?"

Ryan kisses me, a hungry and strong kiss. I guess that means he is okay with the plan. After our usual kissing marathon, we get to eating and watching a movie I ordered, another James Bond movie. We both eventually fall asleep on the couch.

At one point during the night, I wake up feeling cold. I try to wrap Ryan's arms closer to me, but he isn't there. I go in search of him, to make sure he is okay, and hear him on the phone in my room. I don't want to be a snoop, but when I look at the clock it is after one o'clock in the morning. Who could he be on the phone with? Then I freeze. What if he is married, or has a girlfriend, and is calling them from my bedroom while he thinks I am sleeping soundly? I have to hear what he is saying.

"Matt, you don't understand. Everyday I'm lying to her. Everyday she's getting more and more into my heart, and she has no clue who I really am." Then there is a long pause where I guess Matt is talking and Ryan is listening. "Buddy, I think when she finds out, she's going to scream, then get mad, and finally walk away. She's not cut out for this life, my life. I mean, maybe if she loved me she could be. But what if she doesn't wait around long enough to love me? I know I'm sounding like a complete pussy. But you have no idea how amazing she is and how normal this relationship is, and how right it all feels. I don't want to lose her." God, please let him be talking about me. What if I am just a stopping point for him and he is talking about someone else? That would break me, completely and irrevocably break me. I know I already love him. Whatever secret he is hiding doesn't matter to me. But what if I am not the one he is talking about?

"Yeah, if she sticks around, you'll meet her. She agreed to come out to LA for the Thanksgiving break. She's gonna stay with me and I'll tell her then. I think I have to tell her once she gets to the house. How can I hide myself then? Yeah, let me go. I'll see you Monday. Have fun and don't get too wasted. I can't carry your ass home from here. Bye." Ryan hangs up and rubs his hands over his face, like something is really bothering him.

There is one more month until Thanksgiving. I can wait it out that long. I run back to the hallway and pretend that I have just woken up and am in search of him.

"Baby, you okay?" he asks.

"I got a little cold and couldn't find you. Are you okay?" I ask him.

"Yeah, had to use the bathroom and make a call.

Wanna go to bed?" he asks, looking pained.

"Is everything okay? I mean, a phone call at one a.m.?" I ask.

"Yeah, just my friend Matt. He gave me a wasted text, so I just wanted to check on him. But he's fine. Come on, baby, let's go to bed."

I take his outstretched hand and let him lead me to bed. We don't do anything but spoon and fall asleep. The weekend goes quickly. We are just staying in my house and watching movies, fooling around and sleeping and eating. It is magical. I have always been a homebody and don't really love going out or getting too dressed up. I'm most comfortable in jeans or sweats and a t-shirt or tank with my chucks or sandals, and of course my bracelet. The fooling around is great, but Ryan will only do it in the dark with no light coming in, or I can't go under his shirt. I am getting to know his dick better than his chest. Kind of odd, but I am very impressed with the size and girth of his dick, so no worries. We still haven't had sex, but he is a master with his hands and mouth and always makes me cum, so there are no complaints from me. But as good as he makes me feel, I am still scared. Maybe I need to let him know that. Maybe my sharing with him would make him share with me.

Sunday comes and I say good-bye to Ryan, very begrudgingly. I want him to stay. He does surprise me by saying that he'll be back again on Friday. I had figured that, since I am going to be flying to him Thanksgiving weekend and since he made me accept his buying the ticket, we wouldn't be seeing each other until then. How much money do writers make? But if he wants to spend his money, that is fine with me. After all, I get to be with him.

CHAPTER
FIVE

Ryan

The week flew by so quickly for me, which is great because all I want is to get back to Ali. When I land in Vegas, Friday night, I am practically running with Raymond to get in the car. But first a few stops along the way to her. I have to stop and get her flowers, and chocolates, and then dinner. I told her I would get dinner, but the flowers and chocolates are a surprise for all she had unknowingly done. I have been having horrible writer's block for months. But since Ali, I can't stop writing. Not only words, but my music is back. I have barely put down my guitar since I arrived home Sunday night. She is my inspiration. This is it, the weekend I would tell her the truth. I have to. I want us to be able to enjoy Thanksgiving weekend. The only way for that to happen is for me to tell her the truth.

Raymond takes me to a supermarket right near her house and comes in with me while I buy her a dozen red roses. I know, red, really. But shit yeah, she deserves red. Then I go next door to a specialty chocolate shop and buy her a two-pound box of her favorite chocolates, which happen to also be my favorite. Next, Raymond drives me through In-N-Out Burger so I can get a bevy of treats.

I talked to Ali earlier and know she's been having a bad day. I only hope the junk food, flowers, candy and I will make her weekend better. She is waiting by the door when I pull up to her house. I hand Raymond the food, but go to her waiting arms with the flowers and chocolates.

I think she's going to crush the flowers with all the force of her hug. But I love it. I love that she always holds me tight, and never lets go of the hug first. I love that about her. That and so much more. When she pulls back, there are tears flowing from her eyes.

"Baby, what's the matter? Are you okay?" I ask, so concerned for her.

"It's one of my kids. He has cancer. I'm so upset and so scared for him. I feel horrible. I don't know what to do."

"Come on, let's go in the house and we can talk about it." I bring her under my arm and take her shaking body into the house. Raymond follows and puts the food on the kitchen table and makes a quiet exit shutting the door after himself.

"It's my student, Clark. He hasn't looked well lately, very pale, and he's had dark circles under his eyes and this horrible cough. I just thought maybe he was coming down with the flu or something. Then his mom and dad came in for a conference today to tell me that they just found out Clark has leukemia. He's going to stay in school, but he's going to have to go through all these tests and procedures. And there's no one hundred percent guarantee that he'll be okay. I just feel so badly for him and his family. I can't help myself, I can't stop crying."   She is shaking and crying so hard, I'm concerned she might get sick.

She tells me that next weekend she is arranging for the bone marrow donor truck to come take blood samples of people who are willing to be marrow donors for Clark. She asks me if I am willing to go with her. Oh shit. I either have to tell her now, or lie and make an excuse. They would have to know my real name and birth date and everything. I pussy out and lie to her that

I have a business meeting and won't be able to make it into town next week. She understands, but is sad.

I just hold her and rub her back and let her get it all out. When she is all cried out, I ask her if there is anything we could do to help Clark. Is there a toy he's always wanted, a trip to Disneyland, a celebrity he wanted to meet, anything I could do to help him?

"How would you pull that off? I can't have you use all your money for him. You've never even met him."

"I have a friend at a foundation that grants these types of wishes for sick kids. I know you may think this sucks right now, but I can help and you can help me do it. Let's just try not to worry too much this weekend about it, give his family some time to cope and understand it all. Then next week, ask them if there's anything I can do, and I'll make the call. Okay?" I ask her.

"You'd do that for him?" she asks.

"I'm doing it for you, Ali. You're incredible, you know that. I'd do anything for you," I say, and I mean it with my whole heart.

"Since I made dinner cold, do you mind if we talk about something else, something that will probably make me start crying all over again? But it is important."

"We can do whatever you want. Talk away, I'm all ears for you, baby."

"Something happened to me, in high school. Something I think you should know about."

Ali goes on to tell me the whole story of Mitch and what he had done to her. She tells me that after Mitch, she gained weight, first to make guys leave her alone and hopefully ignore her. But they didn't. They still wanted to screw the girl Mitch de-flowered. It became a joke to see who would be next and then next after that. She felt so badly about herself, she slept around and it just gave her a horrible reputation and worse self-esteem. She tells me how her parents were actually mad at her when Mitch dumped her, saying he was her best shot at a husband. They wanted to know what she had done wrong to mess up the relationship. When she told them how it had been a big joke and a bet, they just said it was her fault. She then tells me how she got through college as best as she could, just trying to be a loner, and then she started fresh out here in Vegas.

"But what you have to understand, the reason I'm telling you all this is because there's so much of that young girl that hasn't left me. I'm still very insecure, and being with you isn't a boost to my self-esteem, but a blow."

"Ali, I don't even understand what that means. What are you saying?" I am so confused. I can't believe a guy could be such a jerk and an utter asshole as to take a girl's virginity as a bet. That he could trash her reputation so badly and just walk away as if he was a hero. Didn't he realize what an amazing girl he had in Ali? Although I am momentarily happy that his loss was my gain.

"You're too good for me, and I'm scared for when the day comes and you realize it, and leave. I have really strong feelings for you, Ryan, and I'm really, really scared. Plus, there is more I have to tell you about. A few weeks after the Mitch mess, I was home alone. My parents went away for the weekend because they said that all my moping and crying was driving them nuts.

"I was home on a Friday night. Sarah was out with her boyfriend and invited me along, but three was a crowd. I stayed home and kept getting prank calls all night. Finally, one of the calls was from some guy, it sounded a little like Mitch, but they were whispering so I couldn't be sure. The guy told me I was so ugly and that he heard I was a horrible lay. He said I would make the world a better place if I just killed myself.

"I hung up the phone and went to the bathroom and threw up. I couldn't believe that someone thought I should be dead. I looked in the mirror and thought, maybe they're right. I took out a pair of scissors and slit my wrist. I saw the blood and saw how it was running out of my arm and freaked and passed out. When I woke up, I felt horrible. I felt sick and so sleepy. I called Sarah's house, but her brother Joseph answered. I told him what I had done, and he dropped the phone and ran to my house. He carried me back to Sarah's house, and their parents Gillian and Sam took me to the hospital.

"They stitched it up, but the word got out. I was called "Ms. Suicide Watch" and "freak" and so many other things.

"After I went to that Blacking Out show, I got a tattoo over the scar. That was the first time I met my tattoo artist. He tattooed the words "Just Hold On" over my scar. But I realized that it got more attention after the tattoo, so now I wear the black leather bracelet over it so no one can see it.

"But I don't want to have to wear it around you. I'm not telling you all this to scare you away; if you leave I'll lose it again. But there are times I still get sad and need to cry and feel down and can't control it all. You have to know, it will have nothing to do with you, but there will be times when I'll need extra attention or need to just be alone. Do you think you can handle that part of me?"

She finishes her story and tucks her head down. She looks like a small child, seeming so lost and afraid.

I pick her up and put her on my lap, and wrap my arms around her. I just hold her for a while, wondering if the time has come to open up to her. But I know she had a shit day, and is upset, and since I don't know how she is going to react to what I have to tell her, I can't tell her. I can't hurt her anymore today. I turn her face, holding it in both of my hands so she could look straight into my eyes, and hopefully my soul.

"Ali, I don't want to go anywhere. I'm very happy when I'm with you, and even when we're not together, I'm thinking about you. You have no idea how much you inspire me and open me up. I'm sorry for what that asshole did to you. But I would never do anything to purposely hurt you. You have to look into my eyes and see that truth. I may hurt you, you may hurt me. But it would never be on purpose. I'm crazy about you. And all this shit that I'm better than you, and you don't deserve me, I could kick that guy's ass for ever making you think that were true. If I didn't want to be here with you, I wouldn't be. And believe me when I tell you, there is no place on earth I would rather be than here with you right now. Please believe me, Ali. As far as the depression, I'm glad I know. I have a friend who has manic depression so I do understand the swings. I'm here for you. If I don't notice that it's happening, you just have to tell me.

"And one more thing, baby. Thank you. Thank you for trusting me so much and for telling me. Now give me your arm."

I take the bracelet and unclip it. The scar is still very prominent under the ink. I hold her wrist to my lips and kiss every part of the scar.

Tears are filling her eyes, and I just hope that for now these are happy tears for Ali. I only want to give her tears of joy and smiles. We kiss and then I brush away her tears.

The rest of the night goes smoothly. We eat our cold In-N-Out burgers and fries and also eat about half the box of candy between the two of us. When Ali falls asleep, I go into her kitchen and arrange the roses for her and put them on her nightstand so she can see them when she wakes up.

I take off my jeans and sweater, but leave on my boxers and long sleeve t-shirt and spoon with her sleeping loveliness. It isn't long that I am asleep when I feel hands moving up and down my chest. It feels so good. Then there are fingers grazing along the elastic of my boxers and then, hello, two hands firmly wrapped around my dick.

I don't want to open my eyes in case it is a dream, because God it feels so good. The vice on my dick works up and down, moving me and tugging at me. Then a hand leaves my dick and grabs and tugs on my balls. I moan my pleasure. It is so intense. It feels like I am going to cum any second, but it feels too good to end now. So I start to recite song lyrics and other stupid things in my head to make my end further away.

"That sounded like a good moan. But I bet I can get a better one from you." With that sexy voice of Ali's I know I am not dreaming. I then feel the warmth of her mouth take me in. She is moving one hand on my base, and pumping me, and the other hand is tugging and moving my balls. Her sucks are so deep and strong. Her tongue swirls around the tip of my dick. What brings me closer to the edge is that Ali really looks like she is completely into it and she is moaning more than I am. Each moan brings me closer. I try to pull back from her because I know I am too near finishing. But she shakes her head no in response and just keeps sucking. As my body bows and I start to spurt into her, she locks eyes with me. It is the sexiest thing I have ever done. Looking into her eyes at that moment, as I cum because of her, she knows she has me. She controls me; she owns me. I am hers to have, to hurt, to do whatever she wants with. She pulls back from me, and licks her lips. Then she smiles down at me as I lie on the bed, spent.

I pull her down on top of me, and kiss her hard. She is my goddess. I want to be everything for her. I want her body, mind, heart and soul. I almost tell her I love her. But then I stop myself. I can't tell her when she doesn't know me. I try to feel between her legs, but she pulls away.

"No. Let's get back to sleep. I just wanted to say thanks for the flowers." She smiles wickedly at me and then snuggles back under the covers.

"Shit. If that's how I get a thank you for flowers, what do I get for jewelry?" I ask.

"I don't want jewelry from you. I only want you."

Is this girl for real? God, yeah, I am in love.

CHAPTER
SIX

Ali

The next three weeks, I don't see Ryan. He is busy with work and couldn't come see me. I am busy trying to do as much as I can for Clark. I set up the donor drive and am overwhelmed by how many people showed up. Then I have to set up times to meet Clark at home. He is undergoing treatments and isn't able to stay in school because of how sick and tired he is. I set up little lessons for him and on the days he feels up to it, I go to his house after school to teach him.

We mostly play video games and joke around, not getting too much work done. But it is also a time when his parents can have a break and get out of the house for a while. It feels good to play with Clark and be able to make him laugh and give his parents that break. They are such lovely people, and I can't imagine the hell that they are in.

Ryan and I are constantly on the phone or texting and instagramming pictures to each other. I am just instagramming him a selfie of Clark and me when Ryan calls and asks to speak with Clark himself. I hand Clark the phone and they speak for a few minutes. I can easily figure out the whole conversation. Clark is talking about how he would love to visit Disneyland. Ryan must be asking him what would make this whole mess easier.

When I get back on the phone with Ryan, he tells me my assumptions are right. He gives me a phone number and tells me to give it to Clark's parents to have the whole thing set up. I am so happy that I have to hide my tears from Clark.

Before I know it, Thanksgiving is here and I am at Sarah's house with her parents, her brother Joseph, and her fiancé Michael. My parents don't even call me. But I gave up on my parents a long time ago and am just thankful that I have Gillian and Sam, Sarah's parents, to call my own. Besides, they are better parents to me than mine ever were. Most times I can't even remember that they aren't really mine. And they always make me feel like their own daughter. I begin thinking of what Ryan told me. He said that he had no family and he'd be at his friend Matt's house, with Matt's family. We are even alike in that regard. I don't know if his family is gone as in dead, or just dead to him, like mine were to me. But I am happy he is with his surrogate family as I am.

Sarah, her mom Gillian and I are the cooking team and the men are the watching-TV-wash-dishes-later team. We all work well together and as we cook and bake, we talk about Ryan. Then we talk about Sarah and Michael's wedding. Even though Sarah planned weddings and events for big time companies and major name people, she has been clueless as to what she wants for her own wedding. Gillian and I talked the other day while food shopping for Thanksgiving. We both suspected that things weren't as rosy as they seemed for Sarah and Michael. I thought maybe Sarah was having a hard time getting wedding things together, because maybe deep down she didn't really want to marry Michael.

In the beginning of their relationship, Michael was a dream come true. More recently, he has been anything but. But it is Sarah's decision to make, and my part is to support her.

Gillian and I are having a great time at Sarah's expense telling her all the ridiculous types of weddings she could have. Sarah is always a good sport and even joins in saying she wants a circus themed wedding because we are such clowns.

Just then, as I am laughing my ass off, my phone rings. It is Ryan. I excuse myself to the bedroom to speak to him in private.

"Hey, baby. How is the cooking going?" he asks.

"Great! We should be sitting down to dinner in another half hour. What about you?"

"We already ate the main course, and cleaned the dishes. We're taking a break before dessert. Matt's parents eat early, then we watch the football games, and eat all over again. So this is our break. I'll let you go so you can help. I just wanted to tell you that, at the start of dinner, we all had to say something we're thankful for. I said I was thankful for you. I just wanted to tell you that, baby. I miss you. I can't wait to pick you up tomorrow."

"I miss you too. I'm so excited that I've been packed for days. I'll see you when I land. Bye, Ryan."

"Bye, baby."

Dinner is great and I have the time of my life. I have always been open with Sarah about Ryan's having some big secret. She quickly tells the parents, and we all speculate at dinner as to what he would tell me tomorrow. So the best answers we all come up with are spy, stripper, and escaped convict. Actually I know he isn't an escaped con, because he flies to me all the time. But that is Michael's vote.

After dessert, Sarah pulls me into her bedroom for a quiet talk.

"Look, if this weekend doesn't go exactly as planned, just call me and I'll come get you. I can either pick you up from the airport or I can drive there to get you. I love you and I'm always here. I feel like I don't tell you this enough, but you are always there for everyone else, and I'm always here for you. I hope you know that. I know we didn't both come from Gillian's stomach, but you are my sister, Ali. I am going to hold good thoughts for you that his secret is something totally dumb and stupid and nothing that bothers you at all. I mean, you wouldn't mind if he's a stripper, would you?" Sarah laughs.

I hug Sarah so hard. I wish she were going with me. "I don't think I would want everyone to see my man naked, especially when I haven't seen him completely naked myself."

I have this horrible feeling deep down in the pit of my stomach that Ryan's secret is going to ruin what we have. That's when my idea hits me. I want this weekend to start off well, with a bang you might say. Especially since I don't know how it is going to end. I am going to seduce him before he can tell me his secret. That way, I would at least know I had Ryan. Even if the whole relationship blows up after that, I'll have had his body, and his soul, before I leave to come back to Vegas.

"I'm going to seduce him, Sarah. I'm going to just go with my gut and jump him the first moment I get. Even before he can tell me his big dark secret. That way, if it all ends, I at least had a great shag."

"How do you know it will be a great shag?" Sarah asks.

"Considering how amazing he is with everything else he does to my body, I'm not worried in the least."

The next day, Sarah drives me to the airport, gives me some more encouraging words and hugs and sees me off. The truth is, I must really be in love with Ryan because I hate to fly. I even told him I would rather drive to LA to see him, but he said it would take too long. He did offer to fly to Vegas first and fly back to LA with me, but that just made me feel needy and like a baby. So I start reading the trashy romance novels I put on my Kindle and try to forget the flight and concentrate on Ryan. Thankfully the flight is not bumpy – except for when we are heading out of Vegas, which I know always happens – and it is quick. I arrive before I can fully form my plan. I know what I want to say, and what I want. I want Ryan.

I make my way off the plane and towards baggage claim, where Ryan said he'd be waiting for me. I actually see Raymond before I see Ryan. He is standing behind Raymond and only peeks out from around a large pole when Raymond tells him he sees me. He is wearing a baseball hat, and dark glasses, and is hunched at his shoulders. My smile could light up the whole airport. I am that happy to see him. Then he really shocks me by unfolding a piece of paper and holding it up. It reads, The Woman of My Dreams. I run to him at that point and nearly knock him on his ass as I jump to him. Raymond asks if I have bags as we hug, and when I shake my head no, he quickly ushers us out the door towards the parking lot. Ryan takes my hand, and Raymond takes my carry-on bag and even my purse and very quickly moves us to the car. It is a Range Rover, jet black and with blacked-out windows. Very sexy and very mysterious.

"What would you like to do first?" Ryan asks.

"Actually, I'm a really bad flyer, and was up most of the night worried sick. Do you mind if we head back to your place for a while?" I ask. Step one is almost complete.

"This is your weekend, we do whatever you want," Ryan says as he starts to kiss my neck and then slowly progresses the kisses to my lips.

"Raymond, could you take us home? And then you can have a break for a few hours. What do you say, Ali? What time should we head out to go shopping?"

"How about 5 o'clock? After all, the shops will be

open late from now on because of Christmas, and I don't have too much to get. Sound good? We can be lazy at your place until then," I say.

Ryan agrees, and before I know it the Range Rover is headed into Los Angeles traffic towards Ryan's place. I know from our talks that Ryan has a house but that is all I know. It takes about an hour of driving before we are in front of a set of huge gates. Raymond enters a code at the gates and they open. The house that is facing me is huge and very stately. It is built of dark reddish brown brick. It looks to be either two or maybe even three stories. There are four huge arches on each side of the house, which actually have gargoyles perched on them. The front lawn is very well manicured and there are huge topiaries at the sides of the front double doors. The slam of the gate behind us shakes me out of my awe. What the hell kind of writer is this guy? I guess Ryan really does do quite well for himself.

I thought Raymond was someone he used while he was in Vegas, but apparently, Raymond goes wherever Ryan goes. Maybe Ryan came from money. Maybe he is a stripper. Oh shit, what if he is a drug dealer? Maybe that's why he always tries to cover his face and his eyes and that's why he needs Raymond – he needs protection. That I couldn't stand. I wouldn't sleep with a drug dealer, no matter how badly my body wants him. My heart couldn't take that.

I follow Ryan as he puts a few keys in the locks and opens the door to his home for me. The inside is very well decorated and screams of wealth. You could tell just from looking at the buttery leather black couches that flank the living room. The huge screen TV in the living room is as big as my whole living room.

I just stand there, staring, and in awe. "Want a quick tour before you settle in?" Ryan asks, looking very, very nervous, shuffling from foot to foot.

I just nod my confused head.

He takes my bags from Raymond and tells him to be back at the house at 5:00P.M. Then he takes my hand and shows me to the dining room. It has cream colored walls, and a huge picture of a burning fireball headed to earth. I had seen that picture somewhere, but I couldn't place where and when. I am too overwhelmed to ask Ryan. The huge dining room table is a dark wood and a total square. There is room for six chairs at each side. The chairs are a matching dark wood with red cushions. There are fresh flowers on the table that seem to be blood red orchids. I've never seen anything so beautiful before. Then we walk into the chef-size kitchen. It is all granite and steel. There is a breakfast bar, all brown and cream granite, which hosts six tall back chairs. To the far corner is a smaller square table that matches the one in the dining room. This one only sits eight. The stove is steel and has eight burners, and the fridge is huge and could easily fit two to three people in it. The cabinets are the same dark brown wood as the kitchen table, which is adorned with a small red rose arrangement.

I am too overwhelmed. I am too taken aback. I am scared. But when I turn to Ryan, he looks just as scared.

"I'm getting a bit freaked out here, Ryan. This place is huge. What kind of writer are you exactly?" I ask.

"It's just a house, Ali. I came into some big money and felt like I had to have this place. I'm not sure why. I just saw myself here and it's home. Actually, Matt, my best friend, bought the house directly next door first. Then this one came on the market, and he brought me here. It's just a house. Come on, let's go put your stuff in my room."

He holds out his hand and I take it. He stops in the hallway which has a huge glass chandelier. It looks like the glass sculptures that hang in the Bellagio hotel, by Dale Chihuly. But this one is bright with dark reds twisting and turning to look like an octopus. The floor of the hallway is all marble cream with a brown vein in it. The stairs are off to the right side of the hall and wrap around to the right. The stairs could have come out of *Gone With The Wind*. I have a flash of myself standing at the top of the stairs in a white wedding dress, looking down at Ryan who is waiting for me at the bottom of the stairs. Wow, where did that come from? Five seconds ago, I was about to run from here, thinking Ryan was a drug dealer, now I'm envisioning him marrying me. What is my problem?

I get to the top of the stairs and there is a long hallway ahead of me which has eight doors that I can count. We walk to the farthest door on the left, and Ryan opens the door for me and motions me to go first. I stop short as soon as I enter. There is a huge – and I mean had to be built specially for Ryan – bed at the center of the room. It is an enormous sleigh bed that is a very rich brown that almost looks black, but when the overhead lights hit it, you could see golden hues and then can tell it is dark brown. There are two nightstands, one on each side of the bed. I can tell Ryan sleeps on the right side of the bed. There is a Bose clock radio and his watch on the right side nightstand. The left side has another flower arrangement. A square short vase holds a bouquet of red mini roses. Ryan puts my purse on the bed and my overnight bag on the floor next to the bed. I can't keep my eyes off the bed. This is it. I know we slept next to each other before, and fooled around, but this is it.

The whole room screams sex. I can just feel the sexual tension running through the room. I can picture myself hands tied to the posts of the backboard. I can envision Ryan roughly pulling me to the side of the bed. I can almost taste him in my mouth.

He starts to speak to me and breaks my train of thought.

"I emptied out two drawers for you. I also have

some hangers ready for you. Do you want me to leave you alone so you can unpack?" he asks.

"Seriously, I'm scared that if you leave me alone, I might get lost. Could you just stay here with me, while I take this all in?" I ask.

He smiles and sits down on the bed. Then he flicks on music from his nightstand radio. Depeche Mode starts to play in a low volume. I love them. I always have and I always wished I could see them live. The music soothes me a bit. This is just Ryan. I have to tell myself that he is no different just because it was now obviously clear he has a lot of money.

I kick off my shoes and just drop on the bed with Ryan. He holds out his arms and I crawl to him, resting my head to his chest.

"You have no idea how good it feels to finally have you here. We might have to switch it up and have you here more. But I do love being in Vegas with you. I love your house, and how it feels like home to me. But maybe you should think about getting a teaching job here?"

"Or maybe you should write from Vegas. If you're a writer, can't you write anywhere?" I ask.

"Yeah, actually I can. I do have to stay in town until after New Year's Day. I was going to wait until later to ask you, but do you want to come here for Christmas and spend the holidays with me? I know you probably do stuff with Sarah and her family, but what would you say if we did it just us this time? I could have food brought in, we could watch tons of Christmas movies and do anything else you want. What do you say?" Ryan looks so scared that I might say no. But I have been so scared to ask him if he wanted to spend the holidays with me.

"That sounds like the best idea ever. There are a few things that I would like to add, but we can worry about that later. There is one catch though."

"Anything you want, baby."

"Please don't buy me anything crazy-ass expensive. I mean, look at this house, and you have a chauffeur. I don't want you to buy me anything that will make me uncomfortable. Okay? Just maybe a silly present, alright?" I ask, and plead with my eyes.

"I'll do my best. That's all I can promise. One cheap silly gift. You really are some woman. Now kiss me."

Ryan kisses me, and kisses me until I can hardly breathe. I start to put my hands up his shirt and, as usual, he stops me.

"Don't you have any remote control lights and curtains? Ryan, I have to touch you," I pant.

Ryan

I have to tell her now. That's what my head says, but my dick tells me to close the fucking blinds and lights and just have her. If I have to lose her, I must have her this way before she leaves. I know making love to her would probably break me. If she leaves after that, I am going to be a shell of a man. But this is what I have to have right now; I have to throw those fears away and have her. I do in fact have a remote that shuts the blinds and the lights. I want to have candles lit, but even the glow of the candles would tell Ali the truth. I need us to have each other in the dark. I want to see her beautiful and sweet body. But I have to think of self preservation right now.

I lift the shirt off over my head and throw the hat to the floor. It is pitch black, the only way I can fully sleep. There is no fear that Ali can see my chest. When I reach out for her, her shirt and bra are gone. Skin on skin is the first touch we have. It is electric. Feeling

Ali's huge and soft breasts against my hard chest is like a jolt to my senses. I am instantly hard and it is so uncomfortable against the tight jeans I am wearing. When I start to kiss Ali again, my hands reach for her overflowing breasts. They are soft and her nipples are hard and pin-straight with need. I break my mouth away from Ali's and latch onto her right nipple, playing with her left one in my hand. I suck and bite and tug and hear her moan my name. I hate to admit it, but getting her like this is almost better than when she got me off. When I hear her moan my name, I could cum just like that.

I pull my hand free from her left breast and go to run it down her side, only to find that she is completely naked. There are no pants, no panties, nothing but nakedness. Now I moan. I run my hand down the side of her body. I am on her hip and then running my hand over her hip bone and then I have to kiss her body. I lay her on her back and even position a pillow under her. "I have been waiting since the first night I met you to worship your body."

I continue to kiss her body at her hip. I massage the silky skin of her thighs. I move so that I am between her legs and I can't hold back any longer. I have to taste her. I pull her knees up and move my head just over her pussy. I take a deep breath and her sweet scent fills my nose and makes my hard dick twitch. Her back arches off the bed in anticipation of my touch. I want to hold her still to make the first touch all the more intense. I lay one hand over her belly and hold her down. I use my other hand to open her lips and I lick ever so slowly and gently. She tastes like cinnamon and honey. She is so wet, so sweet and wet. There's something about having a wet woman at your mercy, and knowing you are the one she's wet for. It's insanely sexy and arousing, as if I need to be more aroused than I already am.

I move my finger into her and suck her clit. She is trying to buck off the bed, but I hold her down. She moans my name, and moans for me to add another finger. I do and then rub the inside wall of her pussy. She is close to cumming. She is breathing more quickly and is getting tighter in her walls. I want to feel her cum in my mouth. I want to feel her walls clamp down on my fingers. I want to make her cum and scream my name.

Here she goes, here goes my girl. She cums with a scream and she's shaking.

I slide off the bed. I walk over to the closet and get one of my ties. I bring it back to the bed and crawl back between her legs. She is still having a hard time catching her breath. "I want to tie your hands up," I tell her. Before she can even answer, or I can say anymore, she is on top of me, straddling me with her nude body. She takes the tie from me and very easily wraps up my hands over my head. Then she pushes me back to the bed. She takes off my shoes and socks, then unbuttons my jeans and forcefully takes them from my legs. Then she smoothly slides her fingers into the waist band of my boxer briefs and slowly tugs them down.

"Ali, we can't have sex yet. I have to tell you things first."

"I know you have plenty of things to tell me. But now is not the time. I have a few questions first before I begin to seduce the shit out of you. Question number one. Are you a drug dealer?"

I laugh, but quickly stop as she grabs my hard cock in her hands. "No, baby, not a drug dealer."

"Good. Next, are you an escaped convict?" she asks.

Again, I start to laugh, but then she has me in her mouth. I abruptly stop the laughing. And I have a hard time breathing out the word no.

"Are you a stripper?" She pulls her mouth away from me only long enough to ask the question and then she has me back into her mouth and she's got the right amount of sucking and nibbling.

"No, but if that's something you'd like from me later, I'd be happy to oblige. Oh, baby, that feels amazing."

Then Ali takes one hand away from my cock to feel my balls. She uses them as if they are massage balls and rolls me through her fingers. I am not going to make it much longer. Then she just stops. It is like she pulled all my air away. She is crawling her way up my body until she is hovering over my erect dick. She leans down a bit and uses her hand to pleasure herself with my cock. I freeze.

"Baby, I'm gonna cum soon, let me get on a condom." I roll, taking her with me, and take one from the nightstand drawer. Then she rolls me back and grabs the condom from me. "Are you sure you want this before you know what I have to tell you?" I have to give her the out, even though I am praying she'll keep going.

"Do you really want me to stop, Ryan?" she asks next to my ear and then licks my ear and starts to suck my neck, purposely marking me as hers. I love it. I want a hickey from her. I want the whole world to know I am hers and she is mine. At this very moment, I want to scream it from the roof top. She moves down to use my cock to play with herself again. She has me in her hand and is running me over her clit and making herself moan. Then she lets go and slides further down my body and starts to lick the spot under my sac. That does it.

"Ali, I can't hold out if you do that."

She stops and then I feel the first push over my cock into her cunt. It is so sweet and tight. I can feel at the base of my dick that she is soaking wet. I have to think of song lyrics to make sure that feeling doesn't set me off yet. She slowly slides down, intense inch by inch, just to torture me and herself. I know how wet she is, and that she could just slam down on me, without any pain, but this is better, sweeter. Then she pulls up and slowly lowers down on top of me. I can't hold back any more, so I tell her I'm going to explode any moment. That's when she starts to rock against me and she leans back. I can't touch her because I'm tied and it sucks. She is riding me and feeling my balls at the same time. After only a few seconds, I tell her that I'm going to cum. So she drives me harder and faster. As I cum, I scream out her name and feel my body spasm and lift off the bed. A second later, she is moaning and drops on top of my chest.

She quickly catches her breath and rolls next to me as I remove my condom. But she isn't done with me. She takes hold of my arms and pulls them to tighten the tie and leans her breasts over my mouth and prods me to suck her. I gladly do. Her breasts are amazing. They are huge and real, so bonus for that. Who wants a woman with breasts that are rocks? They move into my mouth so easily and mold to my lips. I am sucking her and she is pulling my arms tighter, trying to give me a little piece of pain. It is getting me hard all over again. She must be feeling the affect she is having on me.

"Tie me up this time, and take me from behind," she says.

Since I only wanted to please this woman, and cum again, I am flipping her over and she is untying me in seconds. Without losing any time, I grab another condom from the nightstand and place it over my cock. I move her hands over her head, and I am tying her hands above her. She hasn't noticed the second ties I brought over. I tie her hands first and then put the second tie over her eyes. I then put the lights on. She won't be able to see my chest, but I can feast on her body. I take all of her in. She is beautiful. She looks like that of an early painting. She is all curves and flesh and silky skin. I was never into bone thin girls. They just had the bodies of little prepubescent boys. What was the point of that? Ali's body is stuff that dreams are made of. I could write sonnets to her beautiful body. I only wish she saw in herself what I see. She has tattoos on her ribs, and I am stunned into silence when I realize that the words are the words of my songs.

I know I have to move, feel her or touch her. I have to do something, to detract her so she doesn't realize that I am stunned by her love of my words. I shake my head and go back to my loving.

I turn her over and start to finger her from behind. She is still so slick and she is rocking her hips back into my hand. She is working herself into quite a frenzy. This is so hot. She is taking what I have to give, even if it is just my hand. I want her. I bring her up to her knees. I take her in a long and sharp deep push. I slide right in, and she is dripping against my balls. I can't go slow, not like she did before. I have to have her hard and fast. I have to mark her. I grab her neck and bring it close to my lips and start to bite her. I know she likes the pain, and she can't help but moan my name. I can't hold out when I hear her voice. I grab her and tell her I'm close. She tells me she is too. I start to think of things to not cum. She has to finish first. I finally hear her scream and then I clamp down and shoot my load.

I let her down on the bed, but don't untie her blindfold. I tell her I am getting a towel to clean her, that I will be right back. She nods. I slip into the bathroom. I ditch the condom and grab a towel for Ali.

I clean her legs and her pussy, drying her off. I want to take a shower with her. But I am scared she'll see my chest and my arms and my ink. So I ask her if she wants me to untie her and let her shower.

"I don't want to wash you away. Is that gross to you?" she asks.

I claim her mouth with mine, letting her know that I

think it is beyond sexy that she wants my scent on her. I feel like a cave man, but I want other men to smell her and know that I'd had her and that she is taken. I pull on my boxer briefs and jeans. Then I put on my shirt and then go to the bed to untie her. I help her get dressed. It is then that I look at the clock. I thought maybe we have been having sex for about an hour, but in reality it's been five. How did that happen? Raymond would be here any second. I grab bottles of water from my mini fridge in my bedroom and rush down the stairs to get ready to go out shopping with Ali.

CHAPTER
SEVEN

Ryan

I never go to a mall, much less with a woman. This is a big and risky move for me. I only hope it will end well. I've made up my mind to tell Ali the truth when she comes back from shopping. I know that she is so looking forward to this outing with me. She thinks the reason I always stay in her house with her is because I am embarrassed of her. She doesn't know that I just don't want anyone to see who I am. I wish I could give her more self-esteem for Christmas. Don't get me wrong, it doesn't bother me. I just wish she could see what I see. It's all this crap on TV and in magazines. It tells women they have to be a stick. I'd much rather eat a meal with a woman than be eating a steak and have them eating a celery stick. What fun is there in that?

Raymond is waiting for us at the front door with the Range Rover doors open and ready. There is a little bit of a chill in the air which is great for me. It gives me a reason to be wearing a hat and a hoodie. How I am going to explain the glasses, who knows. But Ali just seems so happy to be going shopping that I am not going to ruin this for her. We head to the Beverly Center and it is crazy with holiday shoppers. Maybe this is a good thing. Maybe everyone would be so involved in their shopping that they won't even look at me twice. Tons of them are wearing their shades, so again, I am taken care of. It just looks like a lot of holiday shoppers were either up too early, or they wanted to hide behind their eyewear.

The first place Ali drags me to is a book store. Who even knew they still had books? I don't mean to sound uneducated, but I thought everyone did everything digitally nowadays. But this is no ordinary book store. It is a store filled with old first and second edition novels and story books. Apparently Ali's friend Sarah has a favorite children's book and Ali is looking for a first edition. She strikes gold and pays a small fortune for it. Ali researched the mall before coming out and knew exactly where she wanted to go. Next we head to a new age tech store where she buys a cute iPod speaker for her Secret Santa at school. Then we make our way to a small toy store, which isn't like any toy story I had ever seen. These are collectibles and, of course kill me now, there is one with my likeness. That is the one she has to be buying. Maybe fate is against me today. Have great amazing mind blowing sex with the woman of my dreams, a woman I could talk to and be myself around, and then ruin it all by her buying me. I tell her I have to take a call and wait outside the store. That's when my day goes from bad to, holy shit, this day sucks dick bad.

Ali is in the store, buying several different vinyl collectible dolls that represent me and the band members of Blacking Out. That's when I am outside, checking emails from Matt and Jeff. I hear the first gasp of "wow," then know I am done for. Three teenage girls come at me first, asking for photos and autographs. I think I can do it quickly while Ali is still in the store, and then get her out of the mall before it all goes to hell. I give Raymond a nod – he is always nearby, but he is not near enough for Ali to see. Raymond comes rushing over and I am able to take pictures with the girls and sign stuff they have and get rid of them while Ali is still shopping. But as luck would have it, or bad luck I should say, more people see me and see me taking pictures with people, and soon a mob is around and Raymond can't do anything to help. We are two people against a crowd of thirty to forty people and more growing by the minute. Just then Ali comes out and I hear her asking people why there is such a crowd, as she is trying with her eyes to find me but can't.

A young girl, probably fifteen, answers her, "Look, it's Jace Wikks. Here, can you believe it?"

Ali's eyes widen and she starts to look through the crowd. Then she sees me and sees me signing things. She answers the girl back in a laughing voice, "That's not Jace. That's my boyfriend; he only looks like Jace Wikks."

"Yeah, okay sweetie. Like you could nab him. And that *is* Jace Wikks." The girl then physically pushes Ali which makes Ali stumble, and she goes straight down to the floor. Now people are stepping over her to get to me.

Raymond comes to my rescue but I grab him and push him towards Ali. "Just get her out of here and keep her away from the press," I yell to him and he goes right to Ali. He finds her still on the floor. I see him scoop her up into his arms. But she fights him to get to me and get back upon her own feet. I lock eyes with her and see so much hurt and confusion.

"Just go with Raymond please," I plead.

She turns without another word and goes to Raymond. I watch them walk away. She doesn't even look back as Raymond walks her to the car and carries her bags. He keeps a protective arm around her and she lets him.

I am trapped with crazed fans everywhere. Luckily mall security shows up at that point and helps me into the security office. I call Raymond and tell him to get Ali set up at home and make sure she is alright, and then to come back and get me and with a new shirt, because I lost mine. He tells me he will be there for me as soon as possible. So I just sit back in the security office with a crappy cup of coffee and wait for the end of my world.

It takes only a few minutes for Raymond to come into the security room. Why is he here so quickly? "Raymond, what are you doing here so soon? Where's Ali?"

Just then, Raymond moves aside and Ali is standing there with a new shirt and a hurt look on her face.

"Here, cover up those scars," Ali says and hands me the shirt. I am fucked, and not in a good way. She knows and I wasn't the one to tell her. She is going to kill me. If she doesn't, the look of hurt on her face is enough to kill me. Not to mention it looks like someone either hit or kicked her in the face. She has a small bruise on her cheek. This is all my fault. I deserve whatever comes my way. I put the shirt on and hang my head.

"Ali, I don't know what to say."

"I think we should go home and talk about this, Ryan."

With that she walks out of the security room and I am shocked that Raymond follows her and doesn't wait for me. But he did the right thing. I want her protected. Raymond had moved the car so that we would be safely escorted in and out of the mall without a scene or a flashbulb hitting us. We drive back to my place in absolute silence. Ali sits a million miles away from me. She is so close to the other side of the car, I think she might fall out if we hit a turn too fast. She is just looking out the window and I can see her brush away a tear from time to time. It is killing me. I wish she would just yell at me and get this thing going.

We finally get to the glorious gates and the safety of our home. Wait a minute, my home, not ours, but I want it to be our home. But first I have to get out of this hole I am in. We are inside the house and I am carrying Ali's bags. She goes straight to the kitchen and is opening all the cabinets until she finds a wine glass. Then she digs around until she gets a bottle of wine and a wine opener. I don't want to be the first one to talk. I need her to speak first, to see if my lying was not that big a deal, or if she would be walking away.

She gets her wine and then walks to the bedroom and sits on one of the big burgundy chairs I have in my room. She tucks her legs underneath herself and looks so small and fragile with the way she hangs her head and hunches in her shoulders. After she takes a long swig of wine, she puts the glass down and then the reaction she has is one I never would have imagined. She puts her hands over her face, and starts to cry. I can hear the sad moans escaping her hands, and see her shoulders shake.

I am on my knees next to her in a second. I have my arms around her.

"Baby, please don't cry. I hate seeing you upset. Please, let's just talk about this. Why are you sad? I'm still me. I'm still the same person."

"No you're not. You're a rock star. I can't be with you. I'm just a fat school teacher. Don't you see? We have to break up. I can't be with you. I have no self-esteem as it is. To know that I'm one of tons of women you're sleeping with, I can't do that, not even for you. Knowing there are other women, that it's not just me. I can't do it, Ryan. Oh, shit, Jace. I can't do it, Jace. I can't always wonder who you're with, when you're going to find the right woman, and just leave me. This isn't for me."

"What are you talking about? There aren't any other women. And you are not just anything. You are the woman I'm crazy about. Ali, I know it might seem hard to trust me right now, but I swear there hasn't been anyone in so long. I've never been the kind of guy to have a bunch of women. I'm telling you the truth. I'm only with you. I promise you, it's only you."

"Why didn't you just tell me truth when we met? Why have you been lying to me all along?"

"I wanted you to like me because of me, and who I am as a person. You outright said you had a crush on Jace Wikks. I didn't want you to like me just because I am Jace Wikks. I didn't really lie. My middle name is Ryan. I legally changed my last name to Wikks but my real family name is Freace. My real name is Jace Ryan Freace. But now it's legally Jace Wikks. So not completely a lie. Everything I said was basically true. I do write, I do live here in LA. I don't have family, my band is my family. I know I should have told you the truth. But you are normal and have a real life, and I just wanted a normal relationship with you. I kept wanting to tell you, but I was scared that this exact thing would happen, that you would want to leave. Please, Ali, it's still me. Please, don't leave. Let's work through this. I am so happy when we're together. Aren't you happy with me, aside from the Jace Wikks thing?"

"Of course I was happy. But I'm so confused. I don't even know what to call you anymore. Do I call you Jace, do I call you Ryan? I'm so fucking confused. I think I should go back to Vegas and think this whole thing through."

"Please no, please don't leave. Stay here with me. We can just stay in and be us, or if you want, I can show you the sights. I'll do whatever you want, but please don't leave. Ali, everyone always leaves. Not you too." I am so scared that I had to say it out loud.

"What do you mean, everyone leaves?"

"My father left. When the money ran out for his drugs and his booze, he just left. He was home arguing with my mom. He said he had had enough of her and me. He walked out and never came back. I don't even know if he's alive or dead, or where he is. Girls that I've dated, they just always wanted something from me, money, things, getting into clubs or premieres. They never even asked about my past, or parents, or about me. You're the only one, Ali."

"Did you ever even come close to a serious relationship?" Ali quickly looked away after asking me, as if the answer would hurt her.

"I did, once. Melly. She was sweet and had a real interest in my writing and my music. I told her one night about my past, about my parents. A week later, a whole story came across the tabloids about my drug using parents and how I was scared to be just like them. She went to the rag and sold the story because she was mad I hadn't bought her a car she wanted. I closed down after that. I stopped talking again. I have never been great about talking. That's why Matt does all the interviews and stuff. I don't like to sit there and try to explain myself to anyone."

"I have noticed over the years that you never did interviews. I don't remember the story about your parents in the papers, but then again, I don't read that trash."

"It got pulled pretty quickly. I threatened to sue them. I lied and said it was all false. I said I had only told the story to Melly to make her feel bad for me, to get her into bed quicker. So they pulled it really fast and took back the money they paid to Melly. Luckily for me, my parents never tried to cash in on me. But I don't think they're around anymore."

"I don't get it. How do you do anything with all the cameras and people in your face in your life?"

"I don't let them into my life, Ali. I never have let anyone into my life, other than the band, and you. I'm not happy about who I came from, and what they were. It will always haunt me. There are so many unhappy memories stuck in my head. In my own way, I'm just like you, I never feel good enough. I always feel like someone is trying to use me for something. But I know that was never the case with you."

"Still, how do you do anything, how do you go grocery shopping, or go out to a restaurant? How do you have anything normal?"

"It's hard, but worth it, when I can get it. Like when I'm in Vegas with you. We did so much that was normal, because I was with you, because of you."

"I guess there's a part of me that can understand why you did what you did. I guess I was a distraction from what you're used to."

"Stop putting yourself down. You are not just a distraction for me, Ali. I want this to work. I want the whole thing with you. I want what we have. I want us to keep going. Can you please just give me the rest of the weekend to show you that I mean what I say?" I am practically on my knees for her.

"I guess I can see how the weekend goes. But I can't promise anything, Jace. I don't want to be in the public eye. I don't want to be treated like I was at the mall, like I don't belong with you."

"Fine, I'll take the weekend. I'll take whatever you feel you can give me. What do you want to do for the rest of your time here? Just tell me what you want to do or see, and I can have my assistant get it for us."

"Or maybe we should just stay in and have a quiet weekend in. I think I'm done with crowds for a while. Ryan, I mean Jace, I don't know if I can handle this." She stands up and starts to pace. "I am really crazy about you, but I really don't know if I can fit into your world."

"Ali, I only want you in my world. As long as we're together, you fit. I'm so sorry for all this. I'm so sorry this is how you found out. Just give me this weekend to prove to you how much you mean to me, please."

"How can you say that? How can you say I fit in

your world? I don't fit in anywhere. I am a fat stupid, stupid woman who didn't even know who you were? How could I have been so stupid to not even realize who you are? I'm so stupid!"

She starts crying so hard I think she might throw-up. She has to sit back down in the chair to keep from falling down. I want to run to her, but I don't know what to do anymore. I screwed up royally.

I can talk to this woman, about everything and anything. I am only that way with the band and Matt's parents. I actually trust her with my thoughts, and my ideas, and part of my fucked up past. But I don't for the life of me understand why admitting who I am has been such a problem for me. Yet seeing her falling apart like this, this must have been what I have been dreading the whole time.

She doesn't want my money, or my fame. She doesn't even want me anymore. How can I stop this?

"Ali, you have to stop blaming yourself. First off, you are so far away from stupid. I was the one who was stupid. I was stupid for lying to you from the moment we first met. You were just so different. You weren't all over me because I was Jace Wikks. You didn't want my money or connections. You have no idea what it feels like to not be able to trust people, or not knowing if they truly like you for you or for what they can give you or you can give them. You were so sweet worrying about the money I was spending. You were so refreshing. Just so fucking real. You take my breath away, always. Please be mad at me if you have to, but do not blame yourself for one minute. Do you hear me? I made this mess, not you. But please tell me we can get past this. Tell me you'll at least try to stay with me. Because I cannot think of things without you. Please, Ali?"

Ali unfolds her legs and jumps into my arms. I carry her to the bed. I just want to hold her, and that's all we do. I hold her as she cries a bit more from time to time. I try to ease her fears and tell her how much I care about her.

"You have to understand, Jace, even when I thought you were just a writer, I was so scared that you were going to bolt. I couldn't understand why you wouldn't sleep with me. I thought, oh, I thought all kinds of things. But that night, after we went out for French food, and I brought the food to Mrs. McGrath, I thought for sure you weren't going to be back. How can I trust that you will come back to me?"

"I know I really messed up on the whole trust issue. But please, try to look into my eyes and see the truth now. I want you, only you, Ali. The reason I had to walk away from you that night was that I was scared. I saw what a thoughtful and wonderful person you were, and I didn't and still don't think that I deserve you. I would never think to help out someone the way you did. I couldn't get over your thoughtfulness. I had to go back to the hotel and think things through. Truth is I'm just a lost cause, Ali. I'm so scared that you're going to see that and leave. I guess I wanted to just be Ryan for a while."

"But how do I know who I have really been with all long? And what are the differences between Jace and Ryan? You're not the same person?" she asks and looks so shattered.

"I don't know who I am when I'm with you, Ali. I'm like a whole different person. Jace hates to talk to people. He likes his life private. He doesn't like to talk about his crack-head parents and how he didn't speak for years. He just likes to be left alone. But see, that's the thing, since I met you, I love talking to you. I can tell you about my parents and past, and I just want to be with you. So I am having a really hard time figuring all this out myself."

"You trust me with all that? Really?" Ali's eyes are

skeptical.

"I only ever trusted Melly with some of my past and she turned on me. But you, I've already told you so much. I can just see your kindness and I want to be near it, be near you. Please just give this a chance? Sleep on it and see how you feel in the morning." I kiss her forehead and hold her close. She falls asleep so easily, in my arms.

The next day I tell Ali we will do whatever she wants. She says she usually likes to decorate her house on the day after Black Friday. I already have a lighting company working on the outside of the house installing Christmas lights, but instead of the usual decorators, Ali and I are going to decorate the inside of the house ourselves. Because I had planned for a while that Ali would stay with me for Christmas, I had matching Christmas stockings made for the two of us. She is busy putting together a tiny Christmas village set in the living room, when I walk to her with a large black box. I tell her to open it, and tears form in her eyes as she sees the matching Christmas stockings. I am slowly winning back her trust. She knows I want her in my home and, more importantly, in my life.

Even though Ali is scared it will die, we head into town to get a live Christmas tree. There isn't too much fuss made about me, just a fist bump from the teenager selling me the tree. Ali seems relieved. We drive through McDonald's and grab some huge hot chocolates to have when we get home. We decorate the tree with ornaments from the decorator and tons of strands of lights. By the evening, we are bone tired and just want to stay in the house and admire our hard work. We order Chinese food and sit in the living room eating it and watching the soft glowing lights of the Christmas tree.

As we sit by the fire sipping hot chocolate, Ali asks me different questions about my parents and growing up. I answer her honestly, as does she with my questions.

"What was the one toy you always wanted for Christmas and never got?" Ali asks me as we are snuggled on the floor by the fire.

"I wanted several. I remember one really horrible Christmas, though. I wrote Santa a letter in school asking for a toy train, and a little guitar. I brought it to the post office myself. I had asked Matt's parents if I could do chores around the house to earn the money for the letter. I put five stamps on it to make sure it got there. With the rest of the money, I went to the store and bought a box of Christmas cookies and carrots and milk. I went home, and mom was passed out cold in the living room. She woke up as I was putting the stuff out for Santa. She asked me what I was doing. I told her I was leaving cookies and milk for Santa and carrots for the reindeer. She laughed at me. Then passed out again. I prayed and prayed for what felt like all night for Santa to visit.

"When I woke up in the morning, I saw that the cookies weren't touched and the carrots were whole and no milk was missing. But there were presents. So that had me happy. But as I unwrapped the presents, they were my old toys, stuff that had been handed down to me by Matt's parents. Santa didn't come, and that was when I realized that there was no Santa Claus.

"I realized that my mother didn't give a crap about me. No one did."

"I'm so sorry, Jace. I shouldn't have asked you that, knowing you didn't have a good childhood."

"Forget it, what about you?"

"When I was seven, I asked Santa for a Barbie doll. That's all I wanted. I kept asking my mom if Santa would get it for me, and she said if I was good I would get it. So I wake up bright and early on Christmas morning, run for the presents, and there are presents for my mom and dad, and one wrapped box for me, only one. I open it, and it's a book on manners. I looked towards my mom, who was busy opening her tenth box from my dad, and she just shrugged and said she guessed I wasn't good enough for the Barbie. I pretty much gave up on Santa that day, and my parents too. I saw how much stuff they had bought for each other and I was so angry. I remember thinking, why did they even have me?"

Ali and I keep talking while the fire burns. We share more stories of our horrible upbringings. Even though Ali's parents weren't crack-heads, they sucked just as badly as mine did. We have that in common. But we haven't let the way they raised us make us like them. That we have in common too.

The rest of the weekend, Ali and I just stay in. She finishes up her Christmas shopping online on my computer and I do the same. I know what I want to get her, and it would take a bit of time to get it perfect. I would go out to the jeweler when she left to get her special present designed.

When I take Ali to the airport, I am scared. What if she is just going to let me go once she gets on the plane? I manage to get a special pass from security, because the woman in charge is a fan. We wait in a private security area, away from prying eyes. I just keep holding her and kissing her head, telling her I am sorry and to give us a chance.

I know it was all about what that asshole Mitch had done to her. She doesn't know how to get over the fact that I have wanted her, even before she knew who I really am. She keeps calling me Ryan, which I don't mind. When they call boarding for Ali's flight, I walk her to the gate, and kiss her with all the love I have for her. I want to tell her I love her, but it seems too soon, and after all that happened I think it would seem too rehearsed. I want the first time I tell her to be more special than a crowded airport gate with angry people. I have no choice but to let her go. We just let the weekend go, and there is no talk of when I will come see her, and she doesn't push the subject either. I know she needs space and time to think.

But I am going to romance the crap out of her while she thinks about us. I am going to be a dick and make this hard for her. I may be selfish, but now that she is in my world, she isn't leaving. She might not see that yet, but I am not letting her go.

She texts me when she lands, letting me know she arrived safely. That is all I get, which is an hour after she left.

I order a dozen deep red dahlias and have them sent to her and pay a small fortune for them to be delivered to her within an hour of her arrival home. Again, a text thanking me, but nothing more.

The next day I send two dozen purple irises to her work. Again, a text of thanks.

Flowers are not working. So I guess I have to put much more thought into this. The next day I send her three dozen purple roses and a box of chocolates. I get a text of thanks and to stop sending so many flowers, that her house looks like a funeral home. But there is a smiley face after it, so she isn't mad.

The flowers aren't working and the chocolates aren't either. I call a few times, and each time it goes straight to voice mail. She isn't ready to talk to me yet. That sucks. The longer she goes without me, the worse off I am. Then she'll be able to walk away more easily. I have to really think. Ali isn't the type of girl to just want flowers and candy. It would take something grander to win her over. I order twenty-one stuffed animals, teddy bears holding a red heart, and send them to her school, to her classroom. I put on the note that one is for every child in her class, but the biggest one is for her.

Again, a small text of thanks. Nothing is working. I

don't know how to get through to her. I know that I am pacing the floors bare at my house and am having horrible nights' sleep without her. I want to at least know that she is okay and not crying or being sick over this, like I have been.

I call her best friend Sarah and beg her to put Ali on the phone. I had Sarah's number in case there was an emergency with Ali while she was with me in LA. Sarah doesn't even put up a fight.

"I know you screwed up, but I guess I can understand why you would lie to her. She's just really bad about the way she sees herself, and your lying made her feel betrayed. But I think you're worth the fight. I'll get her and put her on the phone. But listen, no more fucking up, hear me? You may be a big rock star, but I can totally have my brother kick your ass if you fuck up again. Got me, Wikks?" Sarah sounds like a good friend, and a scary one at that.

"Got it. I promise you, I'm done lying to her, and just want her to listen to me beg for another chance. That okay with you?" I am almost begging Sarah.

"Sounds good. Let me get her."

I can hear Sarah telling Ali that I have an emergency and need to talk to her. I can hear Ali's sharp intake of breath.

"Jace, is everything okay?" she asks, concern definitely ripe in her voice.

"You won't talk to me, Ali. No, everything is most definitely not okay. I know I'm a shit, but you said you'd think things over, not completely shut me out. I'm coming into town tonight, and I want to see you. Please, I have an appointment at six that's very important, and I want you there with me. Please say yes," I am begging, without an ounce of shame.

"Okay. What time do you want me ready?"

"Be ready by five thirty and I'll pick you up with Raymond."

"I'll be ready. Bye, Jace." She hangs up, not even waiting for my good-bye.

CHAPTER
EIGHT

Ali

It was five thirty before I even knew it. I am dressed in a pair of dark boot-cut jeans that make my ass look amazing and suck in my tummy. The top I am wearing is a Blacking Out tank. I feel like wearing it now that I have no reason to hide who Jace is. Or maybe I just want to shove it to him a bit. I have Sarah do my hair and she makes me look fierce. I have my hair in a high pony tail wrapped with a red bandana and a little poof of a bang. I have a bit of a rockabilly look going on with my huge fake eyelashes. Isn't this what a rock star's girlfriend looks like? Wedged black boots that are under the bottom of my jeans complete the outfit. I am ready, with armor. I have to make him want me, and want to stay. This is how I have to do it.

The bell to my front door rings exactly on time. I open the door to a shy smiling Jace Wikks. He is dressed in hanging dark jeans, a black t-shirt and black leather jacket. He is in fact Jace Wikks, every inch. How did I not see it before? He is hot as hell, and whatever reason he wants me, he does. Maybe I should just try and let my insecurities go, at least for tonight.

"Please say I can kiss you hello 'cause I feel like I'm going to die if I don't." That is all I let him say before I launch myself into his arms and press my mouth to his.

I missed him so much. All my silence had done was make me want to be with him even more. Even if I knew this was going to end with my being hurt, I couldn't take it when he wants to be with me, and I was the one pulling away. It made me want to throw all caution to the wind and hold on tight to my rock star. After all, he is all mine, at least for now.

As we become frenzied enough to do it on the floor, I break off the kiss and look into his eyes. His eyes are smoldering. He wants me. There is no doubt in my mind.

"So, where are we heading?" I ask, very innocently. I like knowing I have him hard and horny and we can't do a thing about it at the moment. He is at my mercy. It might sound bitchy, but whatever.

He takes my hand and leads me to the car where Raymond is holding the door open for me. I say my hello to Raymond and he asks how I am and says that I look very pretty. I see Jace give him a funny look, one that said to back off. Wow. That hasn't happened to me ever, a man feeling so possessive towards me. I like it.

We are in the car and Jace won't tell me where we are going. The car ride is only a few minutes away from my house. We pull up to one of my favorite places, Inked. The best tattoo shop on the West Coast as far as I am concerned. I even know the owner, C.J. He had done four tattoos for me. He is an incredible artist. But what are we doing here?

"Jace, what are we doing here? I like tattoos and all, but I don't want another one right now."

"I'm getting one. It's a Christmas gift for you, but C.J. told me he was going away for a few weeks on the convention circuit and agreed to take me early. I want you to be here for my tattoo. It's for you."

"Jace, no! What, what if it doesn't work out for us? We've only been together for a few months. I'm just getting used to who you really are. You can't get a tattoo for me!" I screamed.

"Are you coming in, Ali, or staying in the car?

'Cause I am getting this tattoo."

With that, he exits the door and walks into the shop, leaving the car door open to me. People are coming out of their booths to shake hands with Jace and some of the customers are taking pictures with him. I look in the mirror at Raymond.

"You should know he's been planning this tattoo for quite some time. At least go see what he's getting, Miss Ali."

I get out of the car and go into the shop.

"Ali, what are you doing here? Want another tat?" C.J. asks as he sees me coming through the door and gives me a big bear hug. Jace immediately comes to my side and takes hold of my waist.

"No, C.J., Ali is why I am here. I'm getting inked for her, it's her Christmas present. Well, actually, one of many. But this is the best one in my opinion."

"Well, I'm glad to see you two happy. This is going to be a great tattoo, Jace. Come on back while I get set up."

C.J. and Jace go to C.J.'s booth and Jace turns and puts his hand out to me. I grab it and smile. Imagine this man getting a tattoo for me. I only hope that it isn't my name. I am not one for name tattoos. C.J. shows the drawing to Jace first, who is smiling so wide you would think he were a kid in a candy store. But then again, Jace is covered in tats, so I guess this is his grown-up candy store. C.J. is getting busy setting up black and white paint cups. And getting his tattoo gun ready. I sit down in the empty chair in C.J.'s station while Jace is busy taking his shirt off and sitting on the tattoo table.

"Jace, you don't have to get a piece just to prove how you feel about me. Please don't do this. It doesn't feel right. You should get inked when you're celebrating something, or for a person as a memorial, or I don't know, but not because you're trying to prove something to me."

"Why not you? 'Cause you aren't good enough? When are you going to get it through your head how special you are? I am not Mitch. I'm really here. Whether you want to stay or not, I'm doing this for you, Ali. This is what you mean to me. Can't you see it? Everyone else can but you. Why can't you just see what this means and how I feel?" His eyes are locked with mine, and they are hurting.

"C.J., could you give us just a minute?" I ask.

"No problem. I'm gonna go call my girlfriend."

I get off the chair and Jace leans up and swings his legs off the table. I step in between them and put my arms around his neck. I kiss his neck, and he kisses my neck back. "I don't mean to be so self-conscious. I just can't see what you see. But I have faith in you. I have so much faith in you. If this is what you want, I'm here, and I'm not leaving. I'm just scared. You have to at least understand my past and what I went through. Plus, like it or not, I'm not the usual rock star chick. You have to at least admit that. You have to at least see why I'm scared. What is it going to be like when you're at a show and all these gorgeous and young skinny girls are throwing you their numbers, or worse, their skinny-ass panties? And here I am, heavy and a school teacher, totally out of my league by being with you."

"You know," he started to shake his head in disbelief, "I wanted to do this, and hoped you would get what this means, that you would say so many different things. But I guess there's no better time or place or way to tell you. I love you, Ali. I've felt it for a while now. I love you. That's why I'm doing this. Because I don't want to stop loving you, and I'm not going to stop. Ever. Even if this gets too much for you, I'm still here. I'll always be here. I'm in for the long haul. Forever. Don't you get that?" He looks so happy to be telling me, and yet so hurt at the same time.

"Are you sure you love me?" I take a deep breath and he nods yes to me. "'Cause I love you, Jace. I love you so much and that's why I'm so scared. I can't lose you. I just can't. It would rip my heart apart and I'd never be the same again."

"You love me?" Jace asks, and looks stunned.

I shake my head yes and then lean in even closer to kiss him. We start to have our hands roaming when C.J. is back clearing his throat. We break apart and smile.

"He's all yours, C.J. Ink away," I say and reclaim my seat. I watch as C.J. makes the outline of what looks to be a bunch of little pieces, puzzle pieces. I don't know what is being put on Jace's arm. But there has been an empty space on his right shoulder. It is about six by six inches on naked, ink-free skin. But C.J. is taking care of that. C.J. and Jace are talking about Jace and the guys going into the studio soon to record their next record. C.J. then brings me into the conversation asking me if I am going to get more ink soon. That's when it hits me that I do in fact want another piece. I tell him I'll talk to him later after he is done with Jace. I don't want to see Jace's piece until it is done, so I keep my eyes on Jace as C.J. is now packing gray, white and black into the outline.

A little over four hours passes when C.J. wipes Jace down and removes the excess ink and lets Jace and I look. It is a world, like a globe, but instead of the states and continents, there are symbols of our dating. There is a bowling pin, a champagne glass, a high heel, flowers – all kinds – and a star, just to name a few. I can't believe it. I look at Jace to see if he is happy with it. His eyes tell me he is totally psyched about it, then he looks at me. As C.J. and Jace talk, C.J. wraps it up with clear film and tapes it down to his arm. I walk over to the tattoo, and take a better look at it. I lean down and very gently kiss it. It is a tribute to us. How could I ever think this man didn't love me? It is obvious he put time, thought and imagination into this tattoo and talked with C.J. over and over about getting things right. I am in love, and falling more and more with every passing second. Jace pays C.J. and I tell him I'll be in next week to go over my next piece. Then we leave and are back in the car with Raymond when Jace asks me if I want to go out or stay in. Screw going home yet. It's Vegas and around ten o'clock. I ask him if we can go to a club and stop by to get Sarah. I know she would love to go out; Michael has a show and she never goes to them, so she would be home. Jace agrees and I call Sarah telling her to get ready, that we are going dancing and that she'll be meeting Jace. She is so excited.

We pick up Sarah a few minutes later and she is ready. Sarah is like that. She could get ready for anything on a moment's notice and look fantastic. Jace asks us where we want to go, and to my surprise I say I want to go back to the club where we met. Between Jace's assistant calling ahead and everyone in town knowing Sarah, we are escorted in without a wait and brought to the VIP section. Jace orders us champagne and tells us to go dance, that he'd watch out for us. Raymond is with us too, to keep the wolves at bay. Away from Jace that is, not Sarah and me. It is obvious by the way we are dancing with each other that we don't want to be picked up, that we are in our own world. No one really bothers us. But my fun is short-lived as women keep trying to make their way to Jace. I see how he dismisses them and then looks to me shaking his head and smiling. That smile. I feel badly for the girls he pushes away. Who wouldn't want to be with him, or even around him? I tell Sarah about the tattoo as we danced. Then we go back to the table for a break. We have champagne, but Jace is nursing his. He grabs me to sit on his lap and kisses my neck.

"Why aren't you drinking?" I ask into his ear.

"I have to be able to make love to your luscious

body later. That is, if you're up to it."

I feel myself getting hot, everywhere. It has been a while since Jace and I have been together. After I found out who he was, he didn't push it and I was confused. Tonight, I am going to rock his world. A girl chooses that moment to come over to Jace and ask if he wants to meet her in the bathroom for a blow job.

"Sweetie, don't you see me sitting on his lap?"

"Yeah, what are you his sister or something?" she asks in a mean girl tone while licking her lips at Jace.

"This is my girlfriend, and get away, now. Or I'll have you booted from the club altogether," he yells at her.

She skulks away, but not before dropping her number on our table. Raymond takes it and says he'll go throw it away. I put my arms around Jace's neck and give him the mother of all tongue fucks in front of the world to see. I do realize lights are flashing our way, but Jace knows better. I think the lights are from the club, but boy am I wrong. They are from people's phones. Hordes of people are taking pictures of us. Why, I couldn't tell you. Why do people care who Jace Wikks dates? Why am I their business? Only his music should be their business. But I guess since I am going to be with Jace, this is just part of the price I am going to have to pay.

I would love to blame it all on the champagne, but who am I kidding. I love Jace and he told me he loved me and got a tattoo to prove it to me. I hold him tighter and just kiss him harder. Let them all see what I have. I have the hottest, sexiest, most talented boyfriend there is. No problem with me if the world wants to see us like this.

"You sure you want to be all over magazine covers and the internet like this?" he asks.

"You fucking bet I do. I want everyone to know

you're mine. You haven't changed your mind now have you? You haven't found a better offer while I was dancing did you?" I ask with a fake pout.

"You are everything that I need and want. There is no one better than you, Ali. I love you." With that I kiss him so hard and long that people flash even more cameras.

"I think it's time we all get out of here. You two need some private time, and I need to ice my dancing feet. Come on," says Sarah.

Jace grabs my hand and then Sarah's and leads us both out of the club.

Raymond drops Sarah home and then we are headed to my house. Of course we have to make an In-N-Out stop first since I want to take away the effects of all the champagne Sarah and I drank at the club. Then we are at my house.

We say goodnight to Raymond and barely make it in the door before we are on top of each other like a second skin. Hands are grabbing at clothes. Clothes are flying to the floor. It is a crazy frenzy of want and need. I have to keep reminding myself to be gentle around Jace's new ink. But when I forget, he doesn't even flinch from my touch. We try to make it to the hallway towards my bedroom, but are stopped by my need. I pull out of the kiss that Jace initiated and push him forcefully against the wall.

"I know you like to talk dirty during sex and I know you like to be in control. But for tonight, let me dominate you. Even if it's just for tonight, be my bitch," I say, very seriously.

I tug on the zipper of his jeans, and pull them down slowly. Then I push his hand away with a smack when he reaches for me.

"You'll touch me when I tell you that you can touch me," I say. Then I pull his long hard dick free from his boxer briefs. I play with his hard cock in my hand for a few short seconds, before dropping to my knees and putting the tip into my mouth and moaning. I love the feel of the smooth skin over his tip and the hard veins that line his shaft. I love the little drop of pre-cum that is at the very end, waiting for me. I lick it up and start to pull him deeper and deeper into my throat. He is too long for me to totally get him all the way in. But I try as far as I can. From his moaning, I know I am getting him off. Then I pull him out and lift his sac and start to lick the bottom, right before pulling him around just so that I can hit his ass. He really loses it, moaning "yes, yes" over and over. As he is egging me on to keep spanking him, I put his hands against the wall and spread his legs as far as they'd go with his pants around his ankles.

"Baby, that feels so good. Please don't stop. Please, make me cum, baby. I need to cum." I smack him and then rub his red cheek. I then grab his balls from behind him and pull them up and lick the soft and hair-free skin of the underneath of his sac. I go back and forth between licking his sac and slapping his ass. I feel him go rigid and grab my hair, pulling my head closer to his sac. I turn him around and he shoots his load all over my bra and chest. I lost my shirt earlier near the front door. I keep stroking him through his orgasm until every drop is out and he is truly done. Then I stand up and tell him to follow me. I walk into the bedroom, go to the bathroom quickly and wipe myself up. Then I crawl on to the bed.

"Strip for me. Take everything off slowly," I order.

His pants, which he had tugged back up with his boxer briefs to walk into the room, are soon sailing down again and off with slow speed. Jace is looking straight into my eyes, never breaking eye contact with me. Then he works off his wet boxer briefs, socks and boots. There he is standing naked as the day he was born in front of me, not moving one step. He is awaiting my next command, which I quickly give him.

"Good job, Jace. Now come here and strip me," I say as I kneel on the bed. I still have on my jeans and socks and bra. He starts on the bra, and kisses my shoulder. I shrug him off me and hold his face in my hands, looking him in the eyes. "Did I say you could kiss me? No, I said to strip me." I lean over and smack Jace's ass. Fear comes crashing over me – what if he doesn't want to play this way with me? I don't like it this way all the time, but tonight I need it. I need to feel in control over Jace, to feel as if I could have all I want with him, even after all he proved to me. But to my surprise, Jace is right there along with me.

He hangs his head, "I'm sorry I kissed you. I'm sorry I didn't listen to you correctly. It won't happen again." He goes back to taking off my socks and pants. Once fully nude I look back at him. He is kneeling on the bed across from me, and he is already getting hard again.

"I want you to suck my tits, Jace. One at a time." I lie back on the pillows and get comfortable. Jace levels himself over me, sure not to let his cock touch me. He played before, a definite turn on. Now he takes hold of my right breast and puts his mouth over the hard nipple. He sucks it into his warm wet mouth. He takes hold of my other breast and starts to pull at the left nipple. I lean forward and give him another smack on the other ass cheek. "I only said to suck them, not tweak them."

"I'm so sorry I didn't listen," he answers.

Then he takes my left breast into his mouth and starts his assault on it. He bites and sucks so hard, I am so wet between my legs. I can't keep the game up any longer. I just want him to touch me and do what he always does so well to me.

"Jace, touch me, please, I'm so wet," I say panting.

"No, Mistress, you have to tell me how and where

you want me to play."

"Just do what we always do, Jace. Please, I need to feel you," I beg.

"No, Mistress, the game's not over yet. Just tell me what you want, and I'll do it. I like this game and I want to play. Keep going."

"I want you to put two fingers in my wet cunt and pump them like you're fucking me."

Jace does not disappoint. He is right there listening and doing all he is told. I am getting so close. I know if we weren't playing the game that I started, he would have his mouth on me right now, rocking me into oblivion. But I started this and he is punishing me, making me ask for all I want.

"Jace, I want to feel your mouth on my pussy. Suck my clit in your mouth and fuck me with your finger at the same time until I cum," I rush to speak before my voice is stolen from me by embarrassment.

Jace does exactly as I ask. His two fingers pump into me with speed, but not like a jack hammer, the way most guys like to fuck a woman. This is with a sure beat of in and out, in and out. There is a magic to his motion. He sucks my clit and rolls his tongue over it at the same speed. I am going to crash into my orgasm so quickly. I can't hold off. I put my fingers into Jace's hair, holding him to my pussy, even though I know he won't go anywhere before I finish. I cum so hard and strong, I think I'm going to break apart into little pieces.

Jace doesn't stop, even after I orgasm, because I haven't told him to stop. "Jace, you have to stop now, I can't take anymore." He immediately stops.

"Mistress, let me fuck you, please. I want to make you come again," Jace says, on his knees over me.

I can't even find the words, so I just nod. He is over me and pushing into me so fast and hard, I think he's going to tear me up. If I wasn't so wet, it would be hurting so badly. He isn't entering me gently at all, but with one thick thrust until he is balls deep into me. I can feel his hard dick inside me, right against my g spot. I am going to cum again. I grab on tightly to his shoulders and mark him with my short nails. The walls of my pussy tighten as he thrusts against me. I feel my whole body tighten and then it feels like I am ripped into heaven as my back bows and my legs start uncontrollably shaking. I cum and can feel the bed getting wet under my ass. Then I feel Jace tighten onto me and a hard scream escapes him. We are both panting and shaking. It takes us a few minutes to calm down. Then Jace rolls off me and holds me tightly to his side.

He turns my face up to meet his and there is such a huge smile on his face, like a Cheshire cat.

"What?" I ask.

"You came for me," he says, still smiling with a wide grin.

"Yeah. I always come for you," I answer, smiling and a little confused why he would say such a thing.

"No, you came, came. Feel the bed. All that wetness is from you, baby. You shot out an orgasm and I couldn't hold back mine once I felt you gush all over my dick. It was the hottest thing ever. I love it. I've never had that with any other woman, just you. You're so unbelievable. I hope you'll believe me one day, and hopefully that one day will be soon." He kisses my forehead and I snuggle closer to him.

I never had anything like this with anyone else. Jace is definitely one in a million, and not just because he is a rock star. No, there is so much more to him than that. His songs aren't merely lyrics and music. They are poems set to music. They are his beautiful voice set to rhythm and motion. They are his laughter, his joy and his anger and pain, all for the world to see and hear. He is that open and remarkable. That got me thinking. If he could show so much of himself to the world, not even knowing them, why couldn't I believe the words he said just to me? I have to try, at least for him. After all, why would he stay with me if I can't accept what he says and what he wants to give me and take from me?

Too much to think about right now. Crazy ass sex and a hot rock star in my bed. I need sleep and dry sheets. But for now, too tired to change sheets. Just need Jace and sleep.

Jace

She is a sleeping angel in my arms. I don't want to wake her. I really don't even want to move to be honest. But I want to write. When the need comes over me, there is no cure except to get out my feelings on paper. I have to bring one of my guitars here to Ali's house. That way, when I want to write, I can work on the music side too. But for now, the words to a new song are breaking against the walls of my brain, begging to get out. The song will be about Ali, but of course only she and those who know her, and know about her, would know that. Matt has been dying to meet her. But I have been skeptical to bring her around to the rest of the band this soon. I know Matt will love her, and that is all I really care about. Members of my band are my brothers, but Matt is more. He is truly the brother I always wanted.

From the earliest memories I have of my fucked up family life, I have memories of Matt. We both grew up in a very upscale area of Marina del Rey, California. The only reason my parents had such a nice home was because my grandmother had money and left the house to her only living relative, her daughter, my mom. My Dad and Mom were both drunks and drug users. They would have sold the home for money if there was anywhere else they could think of going. I don't know the story of how they met, or how or why they wed. But I remember from an early age not to make any noise. I never wanted to make them angry or make them hit me for being in the way. So I was quiet and quick.

I met Matt in kindergarten. He was the only one who even tried to talk to me. All the other kids stopped trying when I refused to answer. One day, in the cafeteria, Matt sat next to me to eat. He looked at me and said, "Jace, I know you don't like to talk, but I figure that makes you a real good listener. That's good for me, 'cause my mom says I never shut up. So, if you want to be my best friend, I'll be yours."

It was that simple for me. He accepted my silence and wanted to be near me anyway. I shook my head yes and then bit by bit I started to speak. Matt always invited me over to his house and little by little I got to be a part of his family. By middle school, I was sleeping over his house all weekend, and by high school his parents helped me get emancipated. I moved out of my mom's house; my dad was long gone. I never looked back. I was a part of his family and that was that. His parents were mine. His family was my heart and whole world. If they didn't like a girl I was dating, she was out before the dinner was over.

When I thought about bringing Ali to meet them, it was funny. I didn't really care if they liked her or not. I only knew that they would in fact love her. They would see how happy she made me and fall in love with her as I am in love with her.

Oh fuck, I love her. But how do I keep her and not have her running? My life is not easy. Does she love me enough to stay and fight? There would be a fight. I know that. Alex, our drummer, had once been really serious with a girl and proposed. The record company blew a fit and our agent nearly had an aneurism. They were so scared that we'd lose fans if we were anything less than wild rock stars. Cecelia, Alex's fiancée, couldn't stand the pressure of pretending she was only a friend and, finally, they called it quits before they got married. So I've been scared about what everyone will say about my being with Ali.

She isn't the usual, heroine skinny, big hair, tons of make-up, dripping in connections, going after my pull or my money kind of girl. She loves the private side of me, and she loves to stay in. We are both homebodies. It's funny, but the only reason we even met was because my agent told me he owed someone a favor so I had to be at the club opening the night I met Ali at. It wasn't her kind of thing either, but she went because of her best friend. Funny, we should never have met. But we did, and now I believe that was fate.

I slip out from Ali's arms and go into the kitchen to find paper and a pen. I make a strong pot of coffee. I start to write. When I notice the sun starting to rise, I open the fridge to make Ali breakfast. There is a package of cinnamon rolls that would do nicely. I pop them into the oven and soon Ali is walking towards me. I guess between the coffee, cinnamon rolls and the wet sheets, she was ready to get up. She looks so cute in her black sweater robe tied at her waist. It only goes to her knees and shows off her beautifully curvy legs and tattoos. Her hair is all messed, like she had just been properly fucked, which of course she had. I smile, knowing I am the reason for her smile and her messed look.

She walks right to my arms, and rests her head on my chest, right over my heart. "I don't know what smells better. You all sexed up, or cinnamon rolls and coffee. Plus there's the benefit that I can eat either. I guess I'll go with your smelling better, since you'll stick around, but the coffee and cinnamon rolls would be gone if I ate them."

I laugh at her way of thinking. It is a good sign that she says she knows I'd still be here. Maybe last night was a breakthrough for her and she now understands how I feel about her. But I know I have to keep telling her the words. She needs to hear them and understand: I am here, forever.

"Ali, I love you. I love you so much," I say and she just sighs into my chest and tells me she loves me too. Then I walk her to the backyard patio and serve her coffee and rolls and we watch the sun rise. We talk about her family and how she never speaks to them, and how Sarah's family is her family now. It is so much like my situation. I always feel like I am unable to be loved because of my family. I mean, when I went to court to ask to be an emancipated minor, my mom never even bothered to show up to court. That was lucky for me, because it told the judge all I had been saying. There was no reason I should have them as part of my life, and they should have no say over my well-being or future. It was at that defining moment when I knew I was messed up. My own mother didn't want me. She wanted her drugs and alcohol more than me. It was refreshing to know I was free of her, but also it broke a piece of me. A piece no woman, no mother figure, would ever fill. I am in fact a bit broken, but right now I don't want Ali to know that.

We talk about the song I have started to write, and about a concert my agent is trying to talk us into doing. I tell her it is in California on New Year's Eve. Then I ask her if she would be my date for the night. She doesn't look too happy about saying yes, but she smiles anyway and agrees. I know all her fears, but I also know they are pointless. I love her. I also know how I will deal with that night. I am going to invite Sarah and her fiancé to come along. Maybe if Ali knows she'll have her own backup she'll feel less insecure. Better yet, I won't tell her about Sarah – I will surprise her with Sarah and her fiancé and then she'll really have a blast. I just have to get to Sarah without her knowing.

After showering and getting dressed, Ali and I head into town to get her a Christmas tree. Even though she fights me, I finally wear her down and she lets me buy her a fake tree. She wants a real one, but since she would be with me for most of Christmas I tell her the tree would be a fire hazard, and with that she relents. We put on Christmas carols and decorate her tree. She even lets me put the angel on the top of her tree. Then we snuggle on the couch and just listen to the music and watch the tree lights dance.

The hours tick by way too quickly. I have to get back to LA for the week, get some writing done and see what my schedule is for the upcoming show. Instead of just Raymond taking me to the airport, Ali comes too. I am a sucker for romantic good-byes, but good-byes when I have to leave Ali suck really badly. I hug for as long as I can and kiss her, not wanting to let her go for even a second. But I do have to say good-bye.

After all, she would be busy with work too. She has finals to get ready, a Christmas party for the class, and her work. Before I leave, she asks me if I would be her date for her school's Christmas party. Of course I say yes. I tell her she has to get a smoking outfit for the New Year's Eve show. I also have to get her present ready. There is a lot we both have to do.

I am able to talk to Sarah and set everything up for her and her fiancé Michael to join us in LA for my New Year's Eve show as a surprise for Ali. Sarah and Michael are even going to stay at my place. It is all arranged. Sarah also has the job of helping Ali get a great outfit for the night here in LA. Ali will be coming out to Los Angeles on December22nd. I have Sarah booked on a flight on December 29th. That means they will be free to shop before the big night. I tell Sarah I want to pay for her dress too, and she is very happy with that. Though she tries to fight me, she very easily concedes to my bossiness and insistence. Even though I feel like I have everything on the right track, I am uneasy.

Ali had said that she always felt loneliest on New Year's Eve. I want nothing more than to make this her best one ever. I want the night to be perfect for her. I hope it will be a night she would never forget. I want all the time we have spent together to be like that, magical and unforgettable.

The flight is quick, and the minute that we land I turn on my phone to tell Ali I landed safely. But my phone is actually ringing as I turn it on. It's my agent. Oh, joy....

"Yes, Allen, what is it? I literally just landed and I'm dead tired."

"Too much dancing with girls I can see. How could you be so stupid as to get your picture taken kissing a fat girl? You're image is being blown to hell. There are already all these tweets and texts going all over that you're a chubby chaser. What the fuck were you thinking?"

"Don't call my girlfriend fat, ass hat. She's not just a kiss or a piece of ass, or anything else unflattering you're thinking of calling her. I've been seeing her for a few months now and I'm not going to stop just because some stupid people think that I need to be dating a stick, no matter what her personality. Allen, you book me shows and work with the record label. That's it. You don't get to say shit about my personal life."

"No, you also pay me to keep you in the public eye, so you can still make millions and millions and enjoy your lifestyle. Now I'm sorry if you don't like the truth, but she's fat and not going to win you points with your fans. End it now. End it before more pictures come to light."

"You're not listening to me, Al. I'm not ending it.

In fact, I'm going to ask her to move in with me. So if you're going to stay my agent and work with me, you better get used to Ali and you better be nice to her. Do you understand me?" I sternly warn.

"Whatever, your funeral," he answers.

I end the call. I would be lying if I said I wasn't expecting his reaction. I knew it would be that way, but I didn't realize it would burn my blood to have someone talk about Ali that way. I always saw myself as a laid back kind of person. I guess when it comes to love, all bets are off. I didn't tell Allen the truth. I'm not going to ask Ali to move in; I'm going to ask her to marry me.

I know it's soon, and it probably is a long shot that she'd say yes without my pressuring her to accept. But I have to ask her. I have to have all of her. I hate when we aren't together. I hate it to the point where I don't think I can breathe without her. I am willing to move to Vegas. I know the guys would love it if we recorded there. Or we can always record when she is on break for the summer and we can stay in the LA house. I know she loves it. I love her place too. There is no reason to get a bigger place, at least not yet. After I knock her up good, we'd worry about that. But one thing I know is that Ali wouldn't just want to give up her job because she was married to me. So I am not going to make her make that decision.

Matt is waiting in my living room when I get home. Matt and I have keys to each other's houses, and Matt does live right next door anyway, so seeing him there is no big deal. But the look on his face is different. I am not going to like this.

"Hey, man, 'bout time you're home. We've all been waiting on you," Matt says.

I hear the other members of the band in the viewing room then. They are watching some kind of sporting event. Sports and I were oil and water, so for all I know it is baseball, basketball, football. All the same shit to me.

"Why are you all so happily present in my house at this late evening? Only good news I hope?" I say, knowing it isn't and hopefully sounding like a complete ass.

"We're all on your Twitter account. I guess that's Ali?" he asks, trying to sound supportive, and failing.

"Seriously, Matt, I didn't expect to hear shit from you. You know I'm happy and you know she isn't like the usual rocker girl. If you're all here to tell me to end it, you can forget it. I'm not going to."

"That's not why I'm here. The others, well, I'm not going to lie. They're not thrilled. You pull in the fans being a free agent and all rockered out. With a chick and a very public relationship, we're gonna lose fans. That's just the way it is, man."

"I didn't know we started this band for the pussy. Why didn't you tell me? I thought we loved music and wanted to share it with people. Maybe I should just leave the band if that's what this whole fucking thing is about!" I yell.

"Wow. What the fuck is going on? You're leaving the band over a chick?" our base player Ian shouted. It seems all the members of the band are now all present and accounted for.

"If you're all going to tell me to end it with Ali, before you even fucking meet her and give her a chance, then yeah, I will leave the fucking band. I thought we were brothers in this. I'm happy with Ali. I even started to write for the new album. But because some cunts don't want to fuck me anymore, then I have to give her up? Do you even know what you're saying to me? This isn't just a fucking passing thing. I want to marry her. Don't you know what that means?"

"Are you seriously going to ask her to marry you,

already?" Matt asks.

I realized it when I had to say good-bye to her this time. I realized I didn't want to keep saying good-bye.

"Yeah. I was going to ask her after the show on New Year's Eve. Or do I not have a gig anymore?" I ask.

"Man, if she means that much to you, I'm behind you. You were always nice to Cecelia. But I hope you remember how that ended and gave this fair thought. I'm behind you, man," Alex our drummer says and comes over to give me a hug.

"Does she have hot friends?" Miles, our synthesizer player, asks and then comes over to me to hug me.

"You know you're my brother from another mother. I just want you happy, and if Ali makes you happy, then I'm happy," Matt says and gets up to hug me.

We all turn to Ian. He remains unmoved. "I'm not going to blow smoke up your ass like these dicks. I don't like this. You're going to change, and then the band's going to change. I'll be civil to her. That's as good as you're going to get," Ian says and then turns on his heels and leaves. The rest of us open beers and toast to my pending proposal.

Then we sit down in the viewing room to watch whatever sports thing they have been watching. I just let the sound of the football, yeah it's football, fade over me. It is all a blur of colors and movement as I stare blankly at the huge screen and think of Ali. Matt interrupts my thoughts.

"Think she'll say yes? Or are you going to have to beg?" Matt asks laughing

"She will think it's too soon, if I know her. But she'll come around," I say.

"If she's not going to say yes right away, why ask now? Why not wait?" Matt asks.

"I want her now. I want her to know I'm ready now. If I know now that it's right, what's the point in waiting?" I ask and smile as I drink my beer.

"I just want to know why she's been such a secret. Why haven't I met her yet?"

"She has really low self-esteem. I have no idea why she can't see what I see when I look at her. So I wanted to wait until she understood I'm not going anywhere before I unleashed you guys on her," I say.

"Well, I saw her picture on Instagram and I think she's hot," Matt says and clinks beer bottles with me.

"Yeah, there's one very big thing to be said about a not too skinny girl," Miles says. "Big tits." I throw a pillow at his head, but he just laughs.

"I think she's very pretty, Jace," Alex says. I can tell this is hard for him. He still isn't over Cece. With that, he says goodnight and leaves.

Miles leaves a little while later, and then it is just Matt and I. When the guys are gone, I feel comfortable telling Matt all about Ali. I even tell him about what that ass hat Mitch had done to her, so he could fully understand why she was so down on herself. He agrees with me to have him hauled out of our show if he ever were to show up.

Matt says that I have to bring Ali by to meet his parents, as if there was any doubt that I would. They are my parents as far as I am concerned. They have to love her like they love me. And I knew they will. How could anyone who comes into contact with Ali not love her? She speaks her mind and is sweet and kind at the same time. She makes anyone feel comfortable. She is everything I want. I just hope and pray that she is ready to accept me and all the shitty baggage that comes along with me.

The next day we all meet up in Matt's house, where he has a make-shift recording studio. Everyone is curious about the new songs I've been able to write since meeting Ali.

I had had a slump. But not a complete block. I had written six songs before I met Ali. But once those songs were written, I had nothing to inspire me, nothing to draw from. The well had run dry. Life was just life, slowly moving and ticking by. Every day was the same.

Then I met Ali and nothing was the same ever again. She brought light to me. She brought heart back to my writing. The five new songs I had written weren't all about love and beauty. Two were about losing the love of your life. I was scared that was what would happen to Ali and me.

The guys hear the songs, and other than tweaks to the music, they love all the lyrics. I tell them that it was hard to write the music while I was at Ali's for lack of a guitar. But they all pull together and we start to work on the music of the first song, straight about Ali, called, "My Light." Ian is surprisingly helpful. He might have reservations about Ali, but he loves her song. I want to work on that one first because I want to be able to sing it on New Year's Eve for her.

We work all day and into the middle of the night. But none of us complains or rushes to leave. This is the fun part for us. Trying to make the lyrics and music work together is hard work, work we all have a hand in. It is what holds us together as a band. It is what makes us brothers.

After that, the days are a blur. We all work hard and relentlessly getting the music and lyrics ready for the show. We only have to play a five song set. But one of those songs would be "My Light" and it would be the first time we performed it together in front of an audience. So we all have to know what the fuck we are doing.

CHAPTER
NINE

Ali

Jace finally flew back to Vegas the afternoon of the school holiday party. I am excited to have him around my school family. He looks hot as hell with his dark hair closely shaved to his head, tattoos and piercings. He is wearing a black button down shirt and black vest over it with tight black pants. He is the man in black, and it suits him just fine. He looks like sin in black. I can tell that he is tired from all the work he and the guys are doing getting ready for the show. But there is something else bothering him. My panicked brain starts to work overtime. Is he embarrassed about my being at the show? Is he reconsidering taking me? Maybe I should make up an excuse and pull out so he won't have to disinvite me.

"Jace, you know, I've been thinking. Maybe I shouldn't be at the show. Maybe I could watch it from home and then we can have our own New Year's Eve celebration when you get home. I mean, you'll be busy and I don't know anyone there. I don't want to be hanging on you and be in the way. What do you say?" I ask, looking sincere.

"No way, beauty. You're coming. I'll take care of you. When I have to go on stage, you can either be in the audience or behind the stage, whichever you prefer. But you're going. Nice try," he says and kisses me.

I introduce Jace to all the teachers and administrators. Then we dance and eat and have a great time. At different times my friends ask if they can cut in so they can tell people they danced with a rock star. Watching him dance with everyone, from my fellow second grade teacher Kathy to the seventy-seven year old lunch lady, warms my heart. This is a side of him I love. He feels that because the public pays his checks, he is theirs. He is gracious and endearing, and really is having a good time with everyone. I made everyone promise no cameras without asking him first and everyone is abiding by my command. He of course does in fact take pictures with everyone. But as the night wears on, I just want him home, in my bed, under me.

When he is finally free and dancing slowly with me in his arms, I whisper to him, "I just want to be in bed with you. Under you to be correct. Just the two of us. What do you say? Have you had enough?"

He smiles and shakes his head and then we start to make the rounds saying goodnight to everyone. I drive home since Jace looks so tired. As we drive I decide to ask him what is bothering him.

"Nothing, baby. Just tired from all the rehearsals. That's all. I promise you," he says.

Before I can ask him further, since I don't believe him, we are at my house.

It isn't long before we cross the door from the garage leading into the house 'til he is on top of me. He is kissing me and touching me. His hands are up my shirt and making fast work on the trouser pants I am wearing. I am only in panties and a bra by the time we kiss our way into the bedroom. Jace tosses me on the bed and then begins to slowly strip out of his clothes. A strip tease show just for me. First, he slowly starts to unbutton his vest and throws it to the floor. Then, slowly and painfully so, he starts to unbutton his shirt. He can tell by the way I am scissoring my legs that I am already getting wet and worked up. He drops his shirt to the floor. Then he starts to unbutton his pants, and stops, eyeing me.

"Slip off your panties, honey," he instructs.

I do as he asks. I slide my black silk boy short panties off my legs and over my butt. Then I throw them at him. He quickly snaps them into his hands, and places them to his nose.

"That's my girl, already wet and ready for me. Have you been thinking about this moment, baby?"

I shake my head in agreement, still moving my legs back and forth.

"Have you been touching yourself while we've been apart?" he asks.

Again, I shake my head yes. "Come give me what I need so badly," I say as I kneel up on my knees, waiting for him.

He shakes his head no. "I want you to show me. Show me how you touch yourself when I'm not here. I'll show you, if you show me." Then he slides his pants and boxer briefs down and stands in front of me nude and hard. He immediately grips himself and starts to stroke himself, looking at my eyes.

I am shocked that I am not embarrassed by the sight of him stroking and pulling at his long and hard shaft. It is doing funny things to me. It is getting me even wetter and I want to cum seeing how beautiful he looks. Without giving it too much thought, I ease back against my pillows and spread my legs, keeping my knees bent. Then I put my hand between my thighs and start to stroke my clit in circles. I am almost lost the moment I touch myself. Jace is such a sight. He is contracting his abs and his neck muscles are bunched.

I pull my breasts free from my bra cups. With one hand, I circle my clit and with the other I pull on my hard erect nipple. It feels good to have the pain pull at my nipple and the tortuous throb between my legs.

"I'm close, baby. But I have to see you come first. Come for me to see," I say through a locked jaw.

I put two fingers into my wet folds and start to touch my g spot and circle my clit with the other hand. I am close. I can't breathe and my back is tight. My face contorts in that mind blowing charge that you get right before your orgasm hits like a tidal wave. I am screaming Jace's name as I cum and waves crash over me. Then I finally open my eyes and see Jace walk over towards me. He pumps his dick with his head thrown back, and he groans a loud growl as he spews all over my breasts. The whole scene is damn sexy. Then when his breathing comes back to normal, he grabs his shirt and cleans me up.

Jace climbs into bed with me and holds me. "I've wanted to see that for so long and trust me when I tell you, it was so fucking hot. I'll never get that image out of my mind. I'm going to use it when I'm on the road and you're not with me," Jace says.

"Planning on leaving me already?" I ask.

"No, never. But I will have to go on tour after the next album drops. But you can come with me. Or come out to see me whenever you want. Let's not talk about it now. It's far off," Jace says.

He holds me and it isn't long until we are both asleep.

When we both wake up it is after one in the afternoon. We have to jump out of bed and rush to get dressed. There isn't even time for us to shower. We have a three o'clock flight back to LA and I still have to stop by Sarah's house so I can drop off her Christmas presents. We are out in the car with Raymond a few minutes later and heading to Sarah's. I drop my presents with her and she gives Jace and me a present in return. That is a sweet surprise for us. Then we race to the airport and Raymond has someone waiting to pick up the car from him, as he helps us through the airport. We have security waiting for us and they quickly move us through the security checkpoint and onto our waiting plane. It is all a fast-paced blur and one I don't know if I will ever get used to, but Jace moves along with such ease. This is what his days are always like – people waiting for him and being there to move him through lines and bending to his every whim.

I am so happy when I finally see the lights of Jace's house come into view. We have the whole holiday to do nothing and everything with each other. I breathe a sigh of relief. When we are in the house, I go straight to the couch and flop down on it. It is only a little after five o'clock but it feels like it's much later. The sun is beginning to set in the late December night. Jace flops next to me and asks what I want ordered in. That's when it hits me. I don't want to have take-out the whole holiday. We need to stuff this house with food and fast.

Jace isn't too thrilled about going out to the grocery store. He is scared that another incident will happen. But I love to shop at the market. I know what I want to cook and what I want in the house. I ask Jace if he wants me to go alone, or he can drive me and stay in the car and wait for me. But he wants to be with me, and I am happy to hear that. I think it will be a good time and very domestic for us.

Going to the supermarket with Jace is so much fun. I love it. I wonder if this will always feel so nice and comfortable with Jace, or if at one point it will be a chore. Then I realize there will be times when Jace won't be able to be with me; he'd be on the road, or off doing interviews and stuff. So this will always be a moment to treasure. We stock two carts with food. I am going to make a turkey on Christmas with all the fixings. Jace is a great chef and loves cooking, so we'll both cook. Lucky for me that Jace isn't one of these crazy just-drink-juice or organic people. He likes to eat – he just balances it by working his ass off. So I feel free to pick up bags of chips and dip. I always go overboard making Christmas cookies, and being here shouldn't change that. So I buy all the ingredients to make cookies with Jace. We definitely won't be starving with the amount of food we buy. We load the car and head back home, after In-N-Out Burger of course for dinner. The great thing about LA is that no one is surprised to see Jace at a supermarket so no one bothers us. Either that, or they don't think Jace Wikks would actually shop for himself, and that's why they all leave us alone.

The next day is Christmas Eve and Jace tells me that he is sorry, but we have to spend some time at Matt's parents' house.

"Jace, they're your family. I want to meet them and spend the whole day with them, just like you would do if I wasn't here. I want to be there. Stop thinking that I hate being around people. I'm just insecure about myself, not about being around others. I'm not a china doll, honey. If you love them, I will love them. I only hope they'll like me."

"How could they not? They'll love you, baby. Just like I do," Jace says.

I have to stop Jace from taking me in the middle of the kitchen. I want to bake the cookies so I will have something to bring to Matt's parents. Jace is a very good sous chef. He does a lot of the prepping for me and keeps me company while I bake. Then we feast on the cookies and milk and, of course, each other.

We go to Matt's parents' house around noon on Christmas Eve. Gloria and Doug Trevinson are instantly two of my favorite people. They hug me and easily welcome me into their home and into their lives. Matt is such a sweetheart too. I can see how close he and Jace are and Matt is trying so hard to make me feel welcome. I help Gloria and Matt in the kitchen and have the time of my life. Gloria and I are busy cooking a ham with sweet potato pie, green bean casserole and salad, all while we sing Christmas carols at the top of our lungs and glug down red wine.

"Okay, you two are too much for me to take right now. I'm joining the men," Matt says and walks to the living room where Doug and Jace are watching TV.

"Gloria, I want to thank you. I kind of know some of what Jace went through growing up. I know you're the woman that raised him. You did a fantastic job. He is so wonderful to me, Gloria. I really feel like I don't deserve him, but I don't want to just spew my fears to you. I want to thank you for all you did for him, you and Doug." I have to turn away quickly because I can see the moisture in Gloria's eyes. I will cry too if she cries.

"Oh, Ali honey, raising Jace was my pleasure and my honor. I'm glad to hear that he's a good boyfriend to you. It means he always listened to me about how to treat a woman. But, honey, it should be me thanking you."

"You're thanking me? Why?" I am truly confused.

"Ali, you have made my son Jace so happy. He has never been this happy before. Not even when the boys got signed. Nothing has ever put such a smile on his face. Look, I know they have a crazy kind of life, and nothing can ever be one hundred percent perfect, but his love for you is. Just always try to remember that, even when it's hard and you guys might not be so close. Okay? He is one of the good ones, and loves you, and so do we. Thank you for loving my son." Gloria hugs me a great tight hug and I hug back, and we are both bawling like mad.

"What the hell, Mom? Why did you break my girl?" Jace asks.

"I'm fine. We were just having a good cry. I think you should cut the two of us off the wine," I say and then walk to Jace to give him a lip smacking kiss.

Gloria is the mother I wished I had grown up with. I

understand why Jace fell so easily into Matt's family. They made me feel so welcome and like I had known them for years. When we sit down for dinner, Doug says a prayer and even makes a point to thank the Lord for bringing me into Jace's life and theirs. I love these people. I silently thank God for them all. All the people around this table are wonderful new additions to my life. I can be myself with these people. I can tell jokes and laugh heartily at theirs.

After dessert, which I helped with too, we make our way to Doug's car and collectively go to midnight mass. I am so happy that the season is not just about gifts and trees. I have so much to be thankful for and I am happy to be going to church with this new family and thank God for them, and also to beg God to keep me with them now that I found them. As we wait for mass to begin, the choir starts to sing the Ava Maria. It doesn't take long for Jace to quietly join in with the song. Hearing him sing, right next to me, is so sweet and touching. Tears silently stream down my face. Jace wipes my tears away. I hold his hand and whisper "I love you" into his ear.

After mass, Doug drops us at Jace's house since we are both a bit tipsy. I go under the tree where our presents are piled and I grab two boxes. I hand one to Jace and I sit on the couch to open the other one.

"I thought we're supposed to wait until the morning to open presents," Jace says.

"It's the one thing that my mother always did right around Christmas. She always gave me Christmas pajamas on Christmas Eve and we were allowed to open them and wear them. So open up."

Jace opens his present and holds up a pair of red and white candy cane striped pajama bottoms with a red Henley top. I open my box and have the top of the matching pajamas of Jace's and a pair of red leggings. Jace smiles when he realizes we are sharing the same pajamas. I thought it was a sweet touch.

"Did your mom ever do anything special and nice 'cause it was Christmas?" I ask Jace.

"There was one Christmas I remember putting cookies and milk and even a few carrots near the fireplace for Santa Claus. I remember waking up the next morning and the cookies were gone with only crumbs on the plate. The milk was gone and the carrots were eaten. She only did it once. The next year, she was too drunk to even leave the bed on Christmas morning."

I walk over to Jace and hold him. When we finally unlock from each other we go into Jace's room and put on our pajamas. Then we cuddle under the covers and put on *A Christmas Story*, his and my favorite Christmas movie.

When I notice that Jace is fully asleep, I go out to where the Christmas tree is lit. I go into the kitchen and crumble a few cookie crumbs on a plate and drink a glass of milk. I put the plate and glass near the fireplace. Then I take a few carrots and leave just the edges near the fireplace. I want Jace to see it when he wakes up. I want him to have a good memory again.

Then I sneak back into bed with Jace, spoon next to him and fall asleep just as Ralphie's friend Flick gets his tongue stuck to the flagpole.

Christmas morning comes with the lovely scent of coffee and cinnamon rolls. I am in heaven. Then I freeze as I open my eyes. Had Jace seen the cookie plate? I jump out of bed and run to the living room and stop short. Jace is sitting by the fireplace and tears are falling down his cheeks as he is holding the cookie plate. I feel like shit. I thought what I had done was sweet, but I guess I should have thought it through. I run towards Jace.

"Jace, honey, I'm so sorry. I thought it would be

cute. I thought we could start the tradition with us and then maybe one day, our kids. I didn't realize it would upset you. I'm so sorry. Please, please forgive me. Please." I am standing over him as he kneels by the fireplace and I am wringing my hands and pacing.

Jace grabs me and brings me into a tight hug. "Baby, this is the sweetest thing. If you give me nothing else but this, I'm happy. They're just tears of joy. Of how incredible you are. I'm also crying for the little kid I was. The one who never got his train set, or little guitar. I'm crying 'cause I want to do this with our kids. They're not sad tears, baby. I promise."

Jace pulls me with him as he settles us by the tree. He puts on the channel that has a full twenty-four hours of *A Christmas Story*. Then Jace goes to the kitchen and gets us both coffee and the cinnamon rolls. After we are relaxed and all smiles again, it is time to open our gifts. The first gift I give Jace is a frame with the first song he ever wrote, "She's Gone." I had stolen Matt's number from Jace's phone and called him while Jace was in LA. I asked Matt to find the song and send it to me, which he did. Then I open my first present, a Louis Vuitton handbag. Wow, not expecting that, but digging it!

Jace's next present is a small silver framed photo of the two of us kissing from his Instagram account, from the night we are out at the club. He holds it to his chest. My next gift is a Louis Vuitton wallet for the purse. Good to have a rich boyfriend! The next is a framed picture of my baby picture and his, courtesy of Matt again. Can you get that framed things are my theme this year? My next gift is a pair of Tiffany sunglasses. Yes, I had seen these in a magazine and I guess looked at the ad too long around Jace. He remembered and bought them for me. The next present I have for Jace is a picture of an empty drawer.

"Is this an empty drawer? Am I looking at the picture right?" Jace asks as he turns the picture all different ways to make sure he is holding it the right way.

"I want you to be more than just a passing guest. I want you to keep things at my place. I want it to be your place, too." He is just stunned into silence. Then he breaks out laughing. Not just simple snickers, a full belly laugh while he rolls on the floor.

"Am I missing something? What the fuck, Jace!" I am so hurt.

He takes my hand and practically drags me up the stairs towards his bedroom. When he brings me into his room, I look around, because Jace had yet to say a word. I keep turning as he looks at the dresser. Finally I get the hint and turn to look at the dresser too. There are three red bows on three of the dresser knobs. "Open them one at a time," he says.

I do as he asks. The first one is filled with my style and size panties and bras. Then I open the second one and there are all color tops and tank tops. The last one has yoga pants of all different colors. All women's clothes, for me. He did the same thing for me as I had done for him. Well, his gift is better because he actually filled the drawers with new clothes for me. It would be nice to get on the plane and just go. Or is this more? Is he asking me to move in? That's what my gift meant. How do I tell him, or ask him?

"You are the most amazing man I have ever met." I hug him.

"I'm not just giving you drawers, Ali. I want you here, all the time. I know that may feel like a lot to take in, and I don't want you to answer right away. Just think about it," Jace said.

"That's the same thing I was asking you, to move in with me," I say.

We pull out of the hug and looked at each other and laugh. We really are meant to be together. But where should that be?

"Let's just not think about it for today. Let's open the rest of our presents," I say and start to walk Jace back to the living room and the Christmas tree. We have a few other silly gifts, clothes and a new pair of chucks I bought Jace. Then we are down to the last two gifts. Jace insists that I open my last gift first. I open the small box and am holding my breath: what if it is a ring? Would Jace really propose this soon? He does want me to move in with him, but that doesn't mean he wants to marry me. But there are things he said about "our kids." Oh shut up girl and open the freaking box. I do and there is the most beautiful necklace I had ever seen. It is a silver or white gold necklace and the hanging pendant is a wrapping bunch of cherry blossoms, and the blossoms have pink gems in them. Knowing Jace and his lavish gift giving, they are probably pink diamonds. He must have had it made to resemble my leg tattoo. It looks just like it. My eyes cloud with tears as I look at him. He is frowning.

"I guess you hate it since you're crying," he says and hangs his head in defeat.

"Are you serious? I love it, that's why I'm crying. How could you even doubt that I would love it? It's my tattoo. But how did you do this?" I ask.

"C.J. has come to be a good friend. He had taken a photo of the tat after he did it. I called him, got the picture and have been working with a jewelry maker for a while. It's white gold with pink diamonds. Let me help you put it on." Jace reaches in the box and takes the necklace. Then he puts it on my neck and leans back to look at it. I turn and run to the hallway bathroom to look in the mirror. It is perfect. I always wanted to have a necklace that was a statement of who I am. Some people wear a cross, or the Star of David. Some women wear their name. I never found anything that was me. This was. I would never take it off.

Then I go back to Jace so that he can open my last gift for him. I sit down and push the huge box towards him. He takes the paper off and lifts the lid off the ginormous white box. Inside is a small toy train set, a bow and arrow set, a small kid's guitar, and a teddy bear. They are all the gifts he had asked Santa for when he was eight – that was the year when Santa never came. Jace looks like a little kid as he riffles through the box and sees all his goodies. I know the reason he really wanted these things was so he could have something to pass to his kids; hopefully, our kids.

"Ali, you are amazing. This is amazing. But you must have spent a mint on this stuff. This is all antique. How did you do this? How did you remember what I had told you?" he asks.

"I didn't spend a mint, I just looked everything up on eBay. None of it is in mint condition I'm afraid. As for my remembering, I remember everything you say. It's all important. You don't say anything unless you want it heard and that's why I'm here, to hear you."

Jace and I curl up on the couch with two mugs of hot chocolate and continue watching *A Christmas Story*. I put the turkey in the oven, but other than that, we barely move from the couch. We stay in our jammies all day and night. In the early evening we have dinner, and then go back to the TV. It is a quiet and sweet Christmas.

I am coming back from using the bathroom when I see Jace sitting near the tree, playing with his trains. I smile and feel such a warm glow in my heart. Maybe moving here wouldn't be horrible. I love Vegas, but I love Jace more. It is something to think about. If it means I will have moments like this with Jace all the time, what would stop me?

Jace

The next day, we plan on meeting at Matt's house for a holiday dinner. Gloria and Doug are going to be there, and although I already had bought them gifts, Ali insisted on buying them something herself. She wants to go with the frame theme. Apparently she has a theme for people every year. We go to an art store and she buys a beautiful gold gilded frame that had a burgundy ribbon for it to hang. Then we go to a copy place where she has a picture enlarged. She won't let me see what the picture is. I figure she took a picture of Matt during the Christmas Eve dinner and is blowing it up for Doug and Gloria. When we get home, Ali locks herself in the bedroom to finish up the gifts and I sit in front of the tree, playing the little guitar she gave me.

I wanted that damn guitar when I was little. But my dad was gone and my mom couldn't care less. She was happy that I didn't talk, so why give me a voice through music? Why let me foster my love of music? That year, she wrapped all my old toys in newspaper and gave them to me. I had to pretend to be happy and grateful, or I'd get a smack. Christmas was always such a mess. Even when I got older and was with Matt's family, it was still hard. They always had tons of gifts for me, as many as Matt had. But they always felt like pity gifts, or charity. These gifts were the first time I remember feeling good about a present. It wasn't the money that Ali spent. It was how she listened and knew what meant a lot to me. Even framing my first song. How did she even think of that? I had kept the paper in a drawer in my desk. I have no idea how Matt found it. And what were the chances we would both give each other drawers?

This woman is my soul. I can't wait to propose. I am deep in the thoughts and images swirling in my mind about proposing to Ali when she walks out of the bedroom dressed to kill. She is wearing a tight burgundy dress that flares at her knees. She has on really high red heels to match and her hair is up, so your eyes go straight to her necklace, the necklace I had made for her. She is a Christmas angel. My angel.

I have a hard-on just looking at her boobs in the dress, barely contained. I kiss her, and she quickly tells me to leave her makeup alone and that she wants to look good when she meets the band at Matt's. I look at the time and realize we'd probably be the last to arrive, so no hanky-panky until we get home.

We walk the few feet to Matt's house and the party is already in full swing. You can hear music and laughter before we even get to the front porch. Ali stops dead.

"Baby, what's the matter?" I ask her, turning to look at her frozen face.

"What if they don't like me?" Ali asks.

"Honey, how could they not like you? Besides, they're all really nice and Gloria and Doug will be there. You have back up. They love you, so does Matt. They told me you were a keeper when you were in the bathroom. They've never said that to me before. Come on, it's fun time. I won't leave your side, promise." I kiss her cheek and walk her forward to the door.

The house is filled with people – not just Matt's parents and the band, but at least one hundred people are here. Most of them are assistants, including my assistant who is making a beeline for us.

"This must be Ali. Ali, my dear, wonderful to meet you," Jeff says and kisses Ali's two cheeks in the air like a true Beverly Hills kiss. "We have to get you some champagne, darling. Oh here, give me those gifts, I'll give them to Lucas, Matt's assistant. Come with me, my dear." And Jeff steals Ali away.

I walk to the kitchen where there is a bar set up and

grab a beer. Before I can even turn away, there is Allen. "Well, where's the woman of the hour?" he drunkenly slurs.

"Ali is with Jeff getting a drink on the patio. And she's not the woman of the hour, but just the woman. Give it up, Allen. You won't win this fight." I walk away. I don't want to hear that I have to be miserable just to make him happy.

"Jace, my dear, where's Ali?" Gloria asks as she hugs and kisses me.

"Jeff dragged her to the patio for champagne. She got you a gift, Gloria. She's been working on it all afternoon, but I have no idea what it is."

"Well, she didn't have to do that. But, honey, I love her so much, I got her a little something too. We'll exchange later. I have to say, son, I'm proud of you. She's a real gem. She's genuine, and sweet, and boy you should see the way she looks at you. Do me a favor, see if she has a sister for Matt and don't let her go. You hear me?" Gloria points her finger at me. Even though she is smiling, she is serious.

"Trust me, I'm working on making her permanent, Gloria."

"That's the boy I helped raise," Gloria says.

"Not helped, Gloria. You raised me. I'll never be able to thank you for all you and Doug gave me. And I don't mean money, or a safe place to live. I found my voice because of you. Thanks, Gloria."

"Do you have to make me cry when I have mascara on? I love you, Jace. You're my own in my heart. Let me go fix my face." Gloria walks off.

A very beautiful and slutty-dressed young woman slithers over to me. But I put her quickly in her place and send her away. A few minutes later, another girl comes my way. This is nuts. I have to find Ali to have these bitches leave me alone. I go out to the patio and there she is, the center of attention with Alex, Matt, Jeff and Lucas. Matt is holding a silver picture frame and keeps hugging Ali. I walk over to the small group.

"Hey, hands off, she's taken." I put my arm around Ali.

"See what Ali gave me for Christmas. Remember this picture, man? She called and we talked for a while and she lied to me telling me she wanted to give it to you for Christmas. I had told her this was my favorite, but that I had to find it. It was in the bottom of a box. Now she had it restored and framed it for me." It is a picture of the band at our first gig. We were all so young, all with ripped jeans and long hair. So different from where we are now. Everyone is laughing at the photo. Her thoughtfulness knows no bounds. She really thinks of everything. She has a way of thinking of the things that would make each person feel special.

I introduce Ali to Miles and Ian. Ian is actually nice to Ali and Miles just kept looking at her rack and then elbowing me his approval. I am gonna kill him. All in all, a great night. Ali is oftentimes the center of the crowd telling a joke or story about her kids, and everyone loves her. The only person who ignores her is Allen. But I take that as a good thing.

As we are about to leave, Ali takes Doug and Gloria aside and presents them with a large wrapped gift. They open it and there is the gold frame she had bought and a photo of Matt and me when we were about six years old. We had our arms around each other's shoulders. The photo was in the center of the frame on a golden piece of thin paper. Around the photo are the words in a beautiful hand, "It is a gift to have two such wonderful sons."

Gloria is in tears, and even Doug is wiping away a stray tear. Then Ali holds both of their hands and with tears in her eyes says to them, "Thank you for the wonderful job you did in raising your son Jace. He's such a wonderful man. I thank you from the bottom of my heart for giving him to me."

Gloria and Doug both wrap her up in their arms. Even I am teary. It is such a gift that she gave them. I am so proud of her. I am proud that she is mine. I leave her with Doug and Gloria while I make one last stop in the bathroom.

CHAPTER
TEN

Ali

"My dear, we bought you a little something too. Here, now open it. But promise me that if you don't like it, you'll tell me so I can exchange it for you." Gloria hands me the box. I open the box and inside is a large Tiffany blue box. I open that box and inside is beautiful Tiffany stationary that has Jace's and my names on it, with Jace's address.

"Gloria, Doug, I don't know what to say, other than I absolutely love it. This is incredible. Thank you so much. But how did you know that Jace asked me to move in with him already?" I ask.

"Ali, the way that boy has been talking about nothing but you, we're surprised he hasn't proposed to you yet." Doug laughs and Gloria gives him a slight nod and poke in the ribs. Okay, weird.

"We're going to go, honey. We have to get some rest and we think that you young ones should party on your own. Now call me if you need anything. Otherwise I'll see you at Jace's house on New Year's Day for brunch. Okay. Love you, Ali." Gloria hugs me and so does Doug as they carry my framed picture out the door. I am watching them leave and don't even realize that there is someone right next to me until he starts to speak.

"So, you must be Alex?" some balding middle aged man slurs to me.

"Ali, my name is Ali," I correct without being rude. After all, this could be the head of the music company, so I better play nice.

"You know, you're really fucking him up, Ali," he slurs out my name and says it like it is a curse.

"What are you talking about?"

"He had over five hundred thousand Twitter followers, and since that picture with you, he's dropped off by twenty thousand. See how you're messing with him? And all because of Corin."

"Corin, who's Corin?" I ask.

"Jace was in love with Corin and she dumped him. He needed to blow off steam so I sent him to Vegas and that night he meets you. You're the rebound, kid. I hate to be mean, but you should know the truth. If you care about him at all, let him get back with Corin. She's beautiful and skinny and his fans love her. You're just bringing him down."

"Excuse me," I say and try my best not to cry in front of this asshole.

I go to the bathroom and don't realize Jace is already in there. So when he opens the door, I run right into his chest. I am shaking.

"Ali, you okay?" Jace asks.

"Yeah, I just had to pee. I'll be right out." I go in and lock the door. I sit on the floor and quietly cry. I knew there had to be a reason Jace was interested in me. I should have known. I'm nothing. This is no better than when I was with Mitch. I am being used again, but this time I am a replacement for someone else.

I know I'm staying in the bathroom too long and Jace is knocking on the door to make sure I am okay. I tell him I am fine in the best fake, tear-free voice I can give. But as I sit on the floor, without even thinking twice I look down at my scarred wrist. I feel like I am suffocating, reliving the pain of my past. I can't live with once again being some guy's piece of garbage or a pawn in someone's emotional game. I don't want to hurt Sarah and her family, but I am losing all my strength. Jace is the one who pulled me out of my depression last time. And if I can't even have that, I'll have nothing. I won't be able to listen to Blacking Out anymore. I can't stand to ever look at his words on my body again. I am having a hard time breathing. I know the thoughts are only moments away from turning into reality.

I should just get it over with. I should just end it all and leave all this pain behind. Whenever I think I'm better, something always comes along to test my strength. Always. But I don't have any strength left this time. He said he loved me, and I told him I loved him. But it was all meaningless – just his attempt to get over someone else. I am again a joke and I am doing nothing but hurting him. I think that hurts me more. It hurts that I know I love him and I am hurting his career, just by being me. I am never going to be good enough for anyone.

I must have really been doing a number on myself. I didn't hear Jace get in the bathroom. I don't notice him until he is on the floor looking at me, as I rock back and forth, and he is cursing and grabbing a towel to wrap around my wrist.

"Fuck, Ali! What the hell happened while I was taking a piss?" he is screaming at me.

The hurtful voice makes me rock more, but stops my crying.

"Nothing, I just feel a little down, with the holidays and all," I lie.

"You're lying, Ali. I know when you lie, you don't look at me. So tell me the truth. And this isn't a little nothing. Look at what you did to your fucking wrist!"

He pulls the towel away and there's blood on it. I look down at my other hand and see that I am physically clawing at my wrist with my nails, causing it to bleed. My rocking halts. I have to get this out and over with. I have to get away from Jace now and be alone.

"Someone came over to me and wasn't very nice. They told me that you were really in love with someone else and I was just a rebound for her. I understand that you didn't mean to make me fall in love with you, but I did, and now I have to leave you, so I'm just really sad. I'll be fine, Jace. You don't have to worry about me talking to the press, or coming back and bothering you. I just need you to take me back to your place so I can get my things. Okay?" I sound dead calm. I know I have to be calm and controlled to be able to get away from him. I know how this works. If he thinks I'm a danger to myself, or him, he'll keep me here with him. I have to be alone and on my own to get away from myself. So I stand up, clean my face and then look at him, ready for the end. But his face holds the look of pure rage and shock.

"Who was it? Was it Ian? Who, Ali? Tell me!" He is shaking me and yelling at me.

"I don't know who he was. He didn't say his name. He was balding and drunk and short," I say.

Jace grabs my arm and walks me around the party until he lays his eyes on the man who told me those things. He marches me over to him.

"Is this the guy?" Jace demands.

"Yes it is," I say in a small voice.

"Allen, what the fuck! What the fuck did you say to her?"

"All I did was tell her the truth. You've lost Twitter followers 'cause of her and you only got together with her because Corin dumped you. Look at her, she's a fat ass. Like this is gonna last?" he slurs.

Jace cocks back his arm, but I grab it and jump on him, taking him down to the floor.

"Don't you hit him, he'll probably sue you," I say.

"See, you just got dropped by the hippo," the asshole laughs and almost spills his drink.

"Please, Jace, I just want to go. We're making a scene." My eyes look back and forth into his. He can see that I don't have much longer to hold it together.

"Yes, Jace, you better follow the herd home. After all, don't want her to sit on you and crush you," he laughs out.

There are others around us, not his bandmates but other guests, and I'm completely embarrassed and want to get away quickly.

"Jace, please, I just want to go home," I beg with tears freely flowing down my face bringing a stream of black mascara with it.

"Allen, get the fuck out!" Matt screams. And then Ian, Alex and Miles are all standing around the weasel.

"Fine, I'll go. But know she's gonna be the ruin of you. She'll make you nothing. I'm the one who made you and she's gonna ruin you," he shouts before Alex and Miles grab him by the arms and literally throw him out the door.

"Ali, are you okay?" Matt asks me, bending down to where Jace and I still sit on the floor.

"Jace, please just take me home," I beg. He finally relents and holds my hand, picking me up as all eyes are on us and everyone is quiet.

We walk home. I go right in to the bathroom. I ignore Jace's pleas to talk to him. I tell him I just want to take a shower. I strip out of my dress and just sit down on the shower floor and have the hot water run over me. I clean off my makeup and just sit there and cry.

When there is nothing left, but empty sobs, I walk out of the bathroom. Jace is sitting on the bed facing the door, waiting for me. He stands as I open the door.

I pull open the drawer and put on a pair of panties and a bra. I then put on a tank top and a pair of yoga pants and socks. I start to walk around the room and put my things back into my luggage.

"Ali, I hope you don't actually think I'm letting you leave." Jace sounds scary calm.

"Jace, I have to go home. Stuff happened tonight, and I just have to go home, get myself together and figure out how I feel about all of this." I continue to pack my stuff.

Jace comes over to me and forcibly pulls the carry-on bag from my hand and throws it down the hall.

"Is any of it true? Am I a rebound for this Corin woman? Are you losing fans because of me?" I ask him.

"I dated Corin for two weeks. She meant nothing to me. Honestly, it was just sex. I know that makes me look bad, but it's the truth and I dumped her because she was an idiot. As far as the fans, no it's not true. My fans are my fans because of my music. If they're fans because of who I'm dating, that's their damage, not mine. Ali, I love you. Nothing is going to change that. Nothing. Please believe me," Jace says as he walks towards me.

"Jace, you have no idea how badly I want to believe you, but I just looked in the mirror and all I have is doubts. All I know is I'm scared and I don't know what to do. I love you and I do believe that you love me. I'm just so scared that your love for me isn't strong enough. That I won't be enough to keep you with me."

"What do I have to do to prove my love to you?

Haven't I done that by asking you to move in with me? I mean, it's not like I'm gonna bring someone else home to the house we share. I introduced you to all my family and friends. They all love you and would never let me ruin what we have. They'd never let me hurt you. Please just try and trust me. That's all I'm asking. Just try."

"I'll try, Jace, I will," I say and hold onto him.

We just go to bed. Jace wants to show me how he feels for me, but I am so tired from all the crying, I just want to sleep. I fall asleep easily, but the sleep is short lived. I have a nightmare about Mitch. I dream that he came to the door of my house and told me that Jace's being with me was just a bet and then he laughed in my face. I stood there crying. The dream wakes me up. But it doesn't wake Jace. I don't want to go back to sleep, even though I am tired. I slip out of bed, careful not to wake Jace. I don't know what to do or where to go. The house is so big. I finally settle on the office. I figure I'll go through my email and clean out my email inbox since I am awake.

Nothing too urgent. Nothing too new. I am still awake and restless. So I do something I probably will regret. I go onto a pop culture site and search Jace's name. There I am staring back at myself with Jace. The comments are far from nice. They are downright mean and hostile. They called me a fat pig. They said Jace was a chubby chaser. One guy said that if he were on a deserted island for years he still wouldn't do me. One woman said I was just trash. The insults go on and on. Then there are tons of comments from women saying that Jace has no taste and that they would never go see the band Blacking Out again. All because of me. Jace lied. I am in fact impacting his music and his band.

I figure out how to get onto a Twitter account and I see that his number of followers is in fact diminishing. I didn't even know he had an account. I never saw him on his phone much. But after I join, I am able to go back and see what he tweeted. There are plenty of tweets about me. He is happy about me. He loves me. He wants to be with me always. They are all nice and sweet tweets about me, about how he could write again because of me. Why don't his fans like me for that?

Then I go onto the Blacking Out website. There is a chat room, and I log in. The true Blacking Out fans are a lot nicer to me. They are happy for Jace. They are happy he is writing again and they are excited about the new album. There is nothing negative. Maybe the true fans really do only care about the music and the rest are just after Jace and pissed he is taken. I am so wrapped up in what I am reading from the fans that I don't hear Jace come into the room.

"Everything okay, baby?" Jace asks, with sleep still obvious in his eyes.

"Yeah, I hope you don't mind I was using your computer. I just wanted to check some stuff."

"Baby, what's mine is yours, always. What are you looking at?" he asks and sees the web site on the screen. "See, the real fans love you. I told you so."

"Yeah, but you lied about the Twitter following. They are dropping off. I'm sorry."

"Baby, I don't even want to be on Twitter. Who the hell has time for it? Allen made us all sign up for an account. If you look at it, I barely ever post."

"I did see that. And you did say very sweet things about me. Thank you."

"Will you come back to bed now? I want you to get sleep. I have a very enormous surprise for you later today and you're going to need all your sleep for it. Come on, baby."

I let Jace lead me back to bed. He starts to spoon with me and then glances at my bandaged wrist. "Did you take your medication tonight, Ali?" Jace asks.

"I did. But they're just a softener, Jace. They don't make it all sunshine and rainbows. I don't want you to worry. I didn't even realize I was doing it." I look at the bandage and it seems like the bleeding had stopped.

"Baby, to think that for any period of time I caused you so much pain that you could do that to yourself fucking kills me. You can't ever do that to yourself again. I need you. Please don't ever leave me, please." Jace looks truly scared.

"I promise to try. That's the best I can give you right now. I'll try to stay and never leave. I love you, Jace. But you have to understand that I'm broken." My chin starts to quiver.

"Ali, you're perfect. I love you, just the way you are. Please, promise me you won't leave me."

"I promise, Jace." I snuggle more closely into him and we both fall asleep.

As Jace and I are eating breakfast in the dining room, the front door opens. I am scared at first, but then think it is probably Matt. But when I look up, there are Sarah and Michael with Raymond behind carrying their luggage. I jump up so quickly that I knock the chair over.

"What are you doing here?" I ask incredulously as I hug her.

"Your amazing boyfriend paid our way out and we're staying with you guys for the concert. Jace knew you wouldn't want to be alone while he was on stage. So here we are. Now finish eating 'cause we're on a mission, girl. We need dresses for the show. And I have just been given Jace's black card to do so as we wish," Sarah says with a huge smile.

I turn to Jace and thank him with a huge hug and kiss and promises of how I will thank him later in bed.

Michael stays behind with Jace, and Sarah and I go shopping with Raymond. Jace insisted that I take Raymond with me for protection. I like Ray, so it is no big deal, but I doubt I need protection. Jace tells me that if there is a problem with the card to make them call the company, that I was added to the account. Again, not bad to have a rich boyfriend with a black card.

Sarah and I find our dresses at the very first shop we come across at the mall. We still love spending the time alone and don't want it to end. I tell her about what happened at the party and how I dug into my wrist and made it bleed. She is freaked out that I have relapsed a bit. But she knows I won't do anything stupid and leave her. I know that even in my darkest hour, I would never be able to kill myself because of Sarah. She would always think it was her fault. I couldn't live with knowing that it would hurt her forever.

Then there is Jace. I do love him with all my heart. I could never leave him with guilt that he somehow had a hand in my suicide. Am I getting over my shit? I don't know. But I want this to work with Jace. I love him and I don't want to leave him.

Sarah says we need more girl time together so we find a salon and get manicures and pedicures. Then Sarah decides she wants to look edgier and sexier and she wants to chop her hair off into a fierce bob. So we arrange for hair styles. I always liked my caramel colored locks, and don't want a cut, but I do want something to make me look a little more rock and roll. So I have several thick bright pink streaks added to my hair. It looks amazing. When Sarah is finished, she has a bright red strip added to her black bob. She looks amazing. Even I would do her with how great she looks, if I were into that.

After finally shoe and purse shopping, we are ready to head home. Raymond is an angel carrying everything for us and even helping us into the house. I hear the music the minute I step in the house, using the key Jace gave me. I didn't realize it before when he handed me the set of keys, but as I put them into the locks of the front door, it hits me. The keys are on a key chain that says "Ali's Keys." He is serious about my moving in. I feel a lump in my throat the size of a grapefruit. I have to face this soon. But today is not the day.

Everyone from the band is in the music room off the viewing room, in addition to Michael. The band is practicing my favorite song, '*Pillow*.' When they finish, I clap and Jace's face lights up when he sees me.

"Ali, where's Sarah?" Michael asks.

"She's trying on her dress to do a big reveal for you. Hi, honey. How was your day?"

"Bitchin' hair, baby. I love it. Truly rock star girlfriend. Now, what does the dress look like?" Jace asks.

"You'll see the dress at the show. No peaking until then," I say.

"TA DA!" Sarah shouts as she comes into the room in her red dress. It is tight fitting and has a halter top. Then it cinches even tighter at the waist and comes right above her knee and has a ruffle mini train on the back. She looks amazing. Given the gawking she is getting from all the guys, even Jace, it's obvious they all agree. "Oh shit, sorry, I didn't realize you had company. Let me go take this off," Sarah says and starts to run away.

"Sarah, wait, it's not company, it's the band. You should meet them. This is Miles, Ian, Alex and Matt," I introduce.

They all come forward to shake Sarah's hand. I notice that when she shakes Matt's hand, neither one of them is too quick to let go. Hum, what is that about? Sarah and I excuse ourselves and go to Jace's room to hang my dress and then I show her to her room to help her out of her dress.

After Sarah changes back to her street clothes, we go back to listen to the guys practice. It is something to watch Jace up close and personal. Imagine playing a CD over and over and feeling that the songs truly spoke to you, and now the beautiful man who made that music is, in fact, singing straight to you. Jace is magic.

I order in about twelve different pizzas – because no one would eat the same kind – for dinner. We all sit around the dining room eating and talking. The guys are great and very nice to Sarah. Michael had gone out somewhere with one of Jace's cars right when I ordered dinner and had yet to come home and see the new Sarah. I am sitting at one head of the table, with Jace at the other. Sarah is to one side of me and Matt is at the other.

"How you holding up after last night, kid?" Matt asks and you could tell in his eyes he is worried.

"I'm fine. Jace and I talked it all through when we got back. I'm sorry if we ruined the party."

"You did no such thing. That douche Allen was the problem, Ali, not you. I'm sorry for all the shitty things he said. I hope you realize the band does not feel that way. You're one of us now. You just keep inspiring Jace to write the way he has, and we'll do anything for you, for life," Matt laughs out.

"So you guys like the new songs? Jace won't let me hear them. He said not until they're recorded."

"They're amazing and you'll love them. In fact, I'll tell you a little secret. We're gonna do one of the new songs at the show. But don't tell Jace I told you. He wanted to surprise you, but I kept thinking, what if she's in the bathroom or something and misses it? It would kill him. So that's the only reason I'm telling you."

"Good to know. Thanks, Matt. Not just for telling me that, but for supporting us."

"Ali, no one has ever made him so happy. Just do me a favor and stick with him. This life can be rough. Alex will tell you first hand. But I think you two can stick it out. After all, I have to keep you around. My parents already consider you their new daughter. That was an amazing gift you gave them last night. You know you didn't have to do that, but they really loved it."

"Look what they gave me. It was the least I could do for them. And I love them too by the way."

Jace

I love to see Ali getting along with Matt. He told me while Ali was out how awesome she is and how we have his full support. He just wants to make sure I will make him the best man at the wedding. As if there is any doubt. As the others come slowly trickling in to my place, they all share the same words of appreciation for Ali. I knew she would win them over, but it is still nice to hear from their mouths. Looking at her at the head of the table, it all seems to fit. She fits in here, she fits in with me, she fits in with the guys. It all flows so naturally. I only hope she sees it too, especially on New Year's Eve.

Everyone leaves after midnight. We are worried that Michael isn't back yet. But Sarah says that Michael often forgets about the time and she is sure he is fine. Sarah tells us that she'll watch TV in the living room until Michael gets home and let him in so we won't be disturbed. We say good night to Sarah and go to our room. That is how I think of it now, our room. Ali starts to take off her clothes and is about to put on a pair of pajamas when I stop her.

"You can't come home to me with sexy rocker hair

and think I'm not going to have my way with you." I push her naked form down to the bed. I stand by the foot of the bed and strip for her pleasure. Then I go to my knees and pull her forward, putting her legs over my shoulders and diving into her wet and delicious pussy. No other woman has ever tasted as good as she does. It is like salted caramel. It is my favorite taste. I am bringing her so close, and I can tell by her harsh breath how into it she is. I love when she is like this, writhing under me.

"Baby, get up here quick. 69," Ali pants.

I jump on the bed as she moves to lie out straight. I am between her wet pussy again, but this time I am hovering over her and she is grabbing my dick and balls with both of her hands. One hand pumps my dick as she puts me in her hot wet mouth. The other hand grabs and strokes my balls. I am getting so close myself. My balls start to tighten under her hands and I am moaning as I circle her clit. She is moaning on my dick and it is creating such a fabulous feeling. I feel like I am going to shoot in her mouth. But I don't want to do that to her.

I'll be honest, I tried my own jiz once when I was a teenager. I just wanted to see what it tasted like. Salt and vinegar, but not like the good chips. I don't want it in Ali's mouth. I like to shoot all over her huge boobs.

I can tell she is about to cum because her breath seems to stop and then shoots out in harsh rushes, and then I put my fingers into her and pump and feel her walls close around my fingers as she cums like a rush into my mouth. I lick her until tears are dripping down her face from the aftershocks. Then I pull free from her grasp and spill myself all over her beautiful tits, giving her a pearl necklace of my cum. She looks so over sexed with lidded eyes and disheveled hair. I love knowing I did that to my girl.

I clean her up and then we climb into bed. I hold her tightly to me and we fall asleep easily. The next day we all climb into the Range Rover and go to take Sarah and Michael to see the sights. It is a very relaxing day and for that I am happy. Ali seems to be at peace with us. She seems calm and happy. Now I just have to figure out a way to keep her away from Allen at the show. I don't want him to ruin the night I have planned for her. I know that Ali is still scared that she is having a negative effect on my career. But as soon as I propose to her, I am sure that all those doubts will be vanquished from her mind.

The day flies and we are all having a great time. That is except for Sarah's fiancé. I love Sarah like a sister already. But I have to say, I don't like Michael. He is never outright mean to Sarah, but there are plenty of snide comments that I catch him dishing to her. Ali notices it too. I can see her furrow her brow every time Michael makes a snide comment to Sarah. He hates her hair, and doesn't have any problem reminding her that it isn't artistic enough for him. She looks great to me, not that I am looking in that way. I take us all out to dinner at my favorite Italian restaurant.

The owner is a good friend. I had been a busboy for him when we were starting out and he would always give me food to take home so I wouldn't starve. Now I am a regular, always leaving a good tip for the excellent service and invariably catering from him when I have a party. Gino welcomes us and we are all seated at the chef's table. I love eating here because the staff knows me and I am not something to gawk at. Bonus is, the patrons don't see me, so no gawking from them either. But Michael isn't impressed. He makes comments about who wants to eat in a kitchen at a restaurant. Sarah tries to steer the conversation and keep it lively so he can't keep the insults going. We talk about what would happen at the show tomorrow. I ask them where they want to watch the show and both Ali and Sarah want to stay back stage, while Michael complains, yet again, that the audience will be more fun.

I want Ali to stay backstage so no one will bother her and Raymond can keep an eye on us both. Then I think how that might be difficult, so I text Ray asking him to see if his wife wouldn't mind watching over Ali. Raymond and his wife Ella both work private security. We have used Ella a lot on the road and she would be a good fit for Ali. Dinner goes on with only minor problems, like Michael complaining when his Carpaccio is raw, even though the menu explains that it is a raw dish. But Ali loves the food and is charming the pants off Gino, which makes me happy. She loves the chef's table. She says it is more interesting to see how the kitchen works like a well-oiled machine. Everyone has a job and they all work well together. I feel the same way. It is exciting to see your food cooked before your eyes.

As we get ready to leave, Gino hands Ali and Sarah cannoli for the ride home. That cannoli gives me ideas. When we say good night to Sarah and Michael, I bring Ali and the cannoli to my bed. I quickly get rid of her clothes and lay her on the bed. I take some of the stiff and sweet cannoli cream and pile it on top of each of her nipples. Then I suck the cream and my girl. I am sucking so hard, she cums just from my nipple work. Then I put dabs of the cream between her thighs and work it up towards her pussy. I eat my way up, and then feast on her. I make her cum a few times and then when she is crying for a break, I give in. I snuggle close to her and hold her as we sleep. I did such a good job, she is asleep in seconds.

CHAPTER
ELEVEN

Ali

The next two days pass quickly. Jace is busy rehearsing with the band. Raymond is taking Sarah, Michael and me around to see the sights. We go to the Chinese Theatre and put our hands in the hand prints of all the famous old movie stars. Sarah and I bought a cheesy map of the movie stars' homes and we're making poor Raymond go driving around and around. Raymond even takes me to see Marilyn Monroe's house where she died and even where she is buried. I buy a bouquet of flowers for her. I think you should always bring flowers to a cemetery.

We are true tourists and even visit Universal Studios to go on one of their studio tours. All in all, Sarah and I have a great time. No matter what we do, Michael is having a horrible time and letting us know he hates everything we do.

Sarah had confided in me that she was having serious second thoughts about marrying Michael. When she told me, I was doing the happy dance on the inside. I love Sarah and will support her in whatever she wants to do. But I am getting to hate Michael more and more because of the way he is treating Sarah, and he hasn't been particularly nice to Jace either.

It is New Year's Eve morning and I am so not thrilled. I never got what the big deal was about this night. All it does it make you feel like crap if you have no one to kiss at midnight. But I do have someone to kiss, and still, I don't get it. Jace is busy in the kitchen, making omelets for all of us while I finish showering off the remnants of last night's crazy, champagne sex. I am dressed in a tank and yoga pants when I go into the kitchen and start to help Jace.

"Happy New Year's Eve, baby," he says and kisses the crap out of me.

"Happy New Year's Eve to you too. So what do we do today? Before the show I mean," I ask, helping get the toast ready.

"I have a masseur coming in a little while to give us all massages. I always get a massage before a show. It's the only thing that helps me get on stage. It relaxes me and pumps me up at the same time."

"I could give you a massage. You don't have to pay someone," I respond and wickedly raise my eyebrows.

"Not that kind of massage, baby. Besides, the last thing I do when you touch me is calm down and relax. We'll all just chill 'til it's time to leave. I don't like to do shit the day of a show 'cause I have to jump around and perform, which takes a lot out of me."

We get the table ready and call Sarah and Michael for breakfast. Michael is still going at Sarah about her hair, but she is just ignoring him by this point. I think she looks great, and besides, to me it is just hair; it grows back, no big deal. I am so happy that Jace is the kind of guy who always supports me, no matter what. I mean, he could have told me I looked like shit with the pinstripes in my hair, but no matter what, even if he hated it, Jace would never hurt my feelings like that. I am very lucky, and I know it.

Sarah and I are clearing the table when Matt walks into the house.

"Hey, Matt, did you have breakfast yet?" I ask him. "I could get you something."

"No thanks, Ali. I ate with my parents this morning. I'm just here to get a massage before the show. You ready for tonight?" Matt asks me.

"I guess, although I have nothing to do but enjoy myself. You're the one who has to work."

"Oh please, what he does is not work," Michael answers.

"Michael, of course it is. Some people would say that what you do, painting people, is not work. Do you agree with them?" Sarah states.

"I work damn hard for what I do, and you don't see me making a mint like he does for strumming a guitar and having people fall at my feet," Michael spits out.

"What Matt can do, hardly anyone else can. Not only does he play the guitar, he sets the mood and he makes the words come to life. He is a true artist. Now if you're going to be an ass, go somewhere else. This is Jace's home. Either respect what he and Matt do, or fly back to Vegas and I'll meet you tomorrow. Make a choice and fucking make it now!" Sarah burns in the eyes. She is truly pissed at Michael and I am glad. I don't want anyone to disrespect Matt or any member of the band. That is Jace's family.

"Well maybe you just want to stay with Matt and be his groupie and I'll just go home."

"If that's your choice, fine, go," Sarah says and turns her back on Michael. Michael storms up the stairs to the guestroom and slams the door shut.

"I'm sorry he's been such as ass, Ali. Lately he hasn't been himself. I don't know if it's the pressure to get ready for his next show, or the wedding. But I am sorry. Matt, please let me apologize for his rude behavior. I think you rock," Sarah says, and with that she goes up to talk to Michael.

"That guy is a prick. She could do so much better

than him. And she's gonna marry that douche?" Matt asks.

"She's telling the truth, he wasn't always like this," I say. "He used to be so sweet and patient and kind. Lately something has changed in him. Maybe it's because he's getting popular in the art world, so he thinks he is who he is. But he was rude, I'm sorry. I know how hard you guys work."

Matt comes towards me and kisses my forehead. "Jace is very lucky to have you."

"No kissing my girl, asshole," Jace jokingly says.

"I think I should try and steal her. Besides, I'm better looking and have more to offer her," jokes Matt.

"Be still my heart, two rock starts fighting over me. Decisions, decisions. I think I'll stick with Jace, but thanks Matt," I laugh.

"Whatever Michael and Sarah are fighting over seems really intense. Know what's going on?" Jace asks.

"Michael is a dick and Sarah told him so. 'Nough said," says Matt grabbing a water from the fridge.

"Seriously, Ali, I think Sarah is amazing, but Matt's right, Michael is a total dick. She needs to drop him. Maybe you can set her up with Matt. Matt, I saw the way your eyes bugged out of your head when she came in with her hot new smoking haircut and dress. Not that I looked, baby," Jace says.

"No worries, honey. Even I would do her she's that hot," I reply.

"She's hot and sweet, but she's engaged, not just dating the douche," Matt states.

"Matt is right. She's engaged," I respond. "I know he seems like a dick right now, but he really wasn't always like this. I think Sarah's right. Ever since he started to work on the pieces for his upcoming show, he's been really nasty. I will tell you that the other day, while we were shopping at the mall, Sarah did tell me that she was having some serious second thoughts about marrying Michael. Guys, Sarah is to me like you two are. We're sisters from another mother. We just have to support her, whatever she decides to do. Got it, boys? But if things with her and Michael don't work out, Matt, I'm all about championing you up to her. Although I do see the way she looks at you. I might not have to do much there."

They salute me and I walk towards Sarah's room. Just as I am climbing the stairs, I see and hear Sarah leaving her room and slamming the door.

"Wanna talk about it?" I ask.

She is holding back tears as she nods her head yes. I take her hand and walk her into Jace's room. When she comes in, she lets out an audible gasp. "Wow, you really did move in didn't you?" she says.

"What are you talking about?" I ask very confused.

"There's a picture of the two of you on the dresser. Your makeup is out and on the dresser. Your clothes are everywhere. This isn't Jace's room, sweetie. It's yours and Jace's. Good. I'm so happy for you, Ali. You deserve someone this good. And I know how much he loves you. It's obvious with the way he looks at you."

"Enough about Jace and me, sweetie. What's going on with you and Michael?" I ask.

"He's packing up to go back to Vegas. I'll talk to him tomorrow when he's calmer. I'm really sorry that this surprise has been a bust. I cannot believe how rude he has been. I don't know what's going on with him. This was the same man who proposed to me in front of dozens of people at his first show. This was the man who'd make me cinnamon toast and tea when I'd come home late from work. This was the man who rubbed my feet after I'd been at a club or event all night. This was the man who, who…. You know, I don't know anymore. That man hasn't been around for a while. Lately he's the man who only wants to be at his studio. He's the guy who never has anything nice to say. He's the person who doesn't want to help me at my events. You know, it's New Year's Eve and I don't want to do this right now. I just want to stay here with you and Jace and the guys. I want to go to the show. I want to have fun with you and dance and drink and when the fucking ball drops, you better kiss me, bitch," Sarah laughs. "Just don't let me do something stupid 'cause he's not here and I'm pissed. I'm still engaged, at least for now. I'm just having me time for a bit."

"I would never let you do anything stupid. That is, as long as you don't let me do anything stupid either. I want to get a little ripped myself and have a good time. I know girls will be throwing themselves at Jace tonight and trust me, even if he's there standing with me, they're not going to stop. Just don't let me skulk away or beat anyone up and start out the New Year in jail. Got it?"

"Pinky promise, sweetie. We'll both have a good time, but watch out for each other," Sarah says as we bond our fingers together.

"Why don't you stay in here until Michael leaves? Jace has a bunch of masseurs coming to calm the band and us too. We can steam in the shower, and then get a massage and then get all girlie together. I can have Jace get ready in your room and we'll get ready here. Sound good?" I ask.

"You sure?" Sarah asks.

"You're my sister. Of course I'm sure. I love you, Sarah. Whatever decision you make with Michael, I'll support you. I'm always here for you. It'll be fun to have girlie time. Stay here and I'll help move Michael along," I say.

Sarah nods and flops back on my bed with the remote control in hand. I go to make sure that Michael is getting out when I hear raised voices coming from the kitchen. Michael is being held back by Jace as he screams and tries to get out of his hold, and Jeff, Jace's assistant, is holding back Matt. They are both fighting over Sarah.

"What the hell is going on?" I yell as I run down the stairs to the impending fight.

"You did all this. Making her come here and thinking she fits in with this bunch of misfits. This is all your fault," Michael screams at me.

"Michael, calm the hell down and stop being a dick. Let me tell you something. I was here in Sarah's life before you and no matter what you two decide to do, I'll still be here. Can you say the same thing? Now go home and cool down and trust me when I say this – you better think about how you acted this week and how you've been treating Sarah. She doesn't have to settle for anyone who would treat her like shit. Now Raymond will drive you to the airport. Go now," I order. Jace releases Michael and then takes hold of Matt's arm and walks Matt to the music room. I wait for Michael to get into the car with Raymond. I tell Raymond to make sure he gets on the plane. Raymond nods and drives off with Michael in the back seat.

Then I walk into the music room where I catch Jace and Matt talking in hushed tones.

"What was that all about? Too much testosterone?" I ask.

"He came down and got into my face," Matt responds. "He said that Sarah snuck out of their room last night and he thought she met up with me to cheat on him. He's crazy. Was I going to stand there and take his shit?"

"Did you sneak out and meet up with Sarah?" I ask.

I don't even know why I am asking, but I have seen the way Matt has been looking at Sarah whenever she is around.

"It wasn't like that. I couldn't sleep and I was in my backyard swimming. I heard someone crying. I actually thought it was you. So I came through the gate that connects both backyards and I saw Sarah sitting by the pool crying. I talked to her for a while until she calmed down. That was it. I didn't lay a hand on her."

"What was she crying about?" I ask.

"Michael. She said that he's been really nasty to her for the past few weeks. She said he's been fine around her family and you, but that while she's been here, he's been mean and she was embarrassed. She was upset that Jace was nice enough to fly them out and pay for a bunch of stuff and here Michael was being a dick. I just let her talk and I helped when I could. That's all. But dickhead gets all up in my face talking smack about how I led her out to the garden to fuck her. I wasn't hearing it, Ali. I hope you're not mad."

"Matt, why would I be mad? Thank you for being there for her when I wasn't. Sarah is my priority, not Michael. And personally after seeing the way he's been treating her and speaking to her, I wish you did knock it with her and we could get rid of good old Michael. But we just have to support her and let her make her own decisions. Jace, I'm gonna steam in the master shower. Knock when the masseur is here, okay?"

"You mean we're gonna steam, right?" Jace asks as he starts to kiss my neck and bite me to mark me again.

"No, honey. I'm gonna steam with Sarah. Then we're gonna get ready together in our room. I know it's not what we normally do. But she's down and I think it'll be fun to have girl time together. You understand, don't you, honey?" I purr and give him a cute pouty face.

"Yes, I understand. But where am I getting dressed?"

"You can use the guestroom, or get ready at Matt's and come back for us."

"We'll get ready in the guestroom. I brought my stuff over here to get ready after the massage. Come on, Jacey, we can have guy time," Matt teases.

"Shut up, you idiot. Come on, Sarah needs me," I say.

"I know, baby. Okay, go have a steam and I'll call you when they're ready for you." Jace kisses me as I run up the stairs to our room. Our room – it does feel like that now, and I really am happy.

Sarah and I have a ton of laughs in the steam shower talking about the guys. I am talking about Jace and our wild sex life and she is surprisingly talking about Matt. She tells me how he found her by the pool and stayed with her until the sun started to rise. She says that if things were to be different, she could definitely see herself with someone like Matt, but she still isn't sure what she wants to do with Michael yet. I would love setting her up with Matt. Not only would they make a gorgeous couple, but they are both sweet and caring people. Sarah and her family had given me a family when my biological parents turned their backs on me. Matt and his family had done the same for Jace.

But I have to respect what Sarah is saying and not put my two cents in. I just need to be there for her, however she needs me, just like she is always there for me. We finish our steams and get ready for our massages. I give Sarah one of Jace's many robes. Does my boyfriend think he is Hugh Heffner? I put one on too and we are just talking, waiting for someone to tell us that it is our turn. Jeff comes in a few moments later to tell us that the guys are just about done, and it will soon be our turn, so we should go downstairs.

When we get down the stairs, the guys are just getting up off the massage tables. I only have eyes for Jace and his ripped chest. But then I hear Sarah's quick intake of breath and look to where her eyes are focused. Oh hell, Matt looks amazing. He is sitting with his legs off the table, dangling, and he has only a small white towel wrapped around his waist. He is texting someone on his phone and doesn't even look up. But I think he knows Sarah is watching him. I see his muscles really flexing.

"Um, baby? Eyes on me, sweetheart," Jace teases me.

I shake my head from the Matt sexiness fog, and turn back to Jace.

"Have you two always had bodies like this? That is just not fair to the female sex," I say and look my honey up and down as he is standing next to the massage table he just jumped off, also wrapped in nothing else but a small white towel.

"Actually, yes, we've always enjoyed working out," Jace says and purposely flexes his chest muscles at me.

"Okay, men, get going upstairs and steam. It's the ladies' turn. Now, Ali, you take this one; Sarah, you go here. Upstairs, boys. The ladies have to disrobe," Jeff tells the guys and physically moves the boys towards the stairs. The guys are laughing, but I can tell neither Jace nor Matt really wants to move away from Sarah and me.

"Take care of our girls while we're steaming, Jeff," Jace orders Jeff.

Sarah leans over to me. "Did he just say 'our' girls?" Sarah asks, but doesn't sound upset about Jace's choice of words.

"I don't have proof, but I do think Matt has a crush on you," I whisper to Sarah so no one can hear.

"Really?" Sarah responds and turns a little red, with

a smile on her face.

Sarah jumps up to her massage table and pulls the robe off at the same time that I do. We both start out face down and are instantly moaning from the massages. Sarah and I like periodically going to the spa and having a day of relaxation when we're home. We usually do it twice a year. But all of those massages pale in comparison. I am moaning so loudly that before I know it, I hear giggling and look up to see Jace and Matt at the top of the stairs looking down at Sarah and me.

"I can't help it. Maddy is amazing. We should just hire her to live here with us," I flop back and yell up to Jace.

"Here with us? Does that mean that you've answered my question?" Jace asks.

"I guess I did. But can we work out logistics later? I have to give Maddy my full attention. Now go back and steam while I fall more in love with Maddy." I continue to moan at the best hands I've ever had on my body, aside from Jace's that is.

It's over an hour and I have fallen asleep when Jeff whispers into my ear that the massage is over and it's time to get ready. I grudgingly lift myself from the table and wrap the robe around myself. I look totally sleepy and relaxed, and so does Sarah.

We both slowly as snails walk up to Jace's and my bedroom and just sit down on the bed. We are too relaxed to even think about moving. But then a tornado by the name of Jeff comes in to turn us upside down.

"Okay, ladies, I have some champagne to get this girls' party started. I am here to do your hair and makeup my dears. So, just sit back, drink up and relax." Jeff moves Sarah to the chair at the makeup table Jace had bought me.

Jeff hands Sarah a glass of champagne and starts to run a brush through her sleep-rumpled hair. She downs the first glass without coming up for air and holds it out toward me for a refill, which I give her.

"So, Sarah, pretty awesome to have two great artists fighting over you, huh?" Jeff asks Sarah.

"What do you mean two artists fighting over me?" she asks.

"Well, the way I hear it, your fiancé was bad mouthing you to Matt and he threw a punch. That's when I came in and I grabbed Matt and Jace grabbed Michael before he could swing back. Matt was so pissed I held him. To be honest, I was surprised I was able to hold him off your man. Matt is cut. Too bad he's batting for the wrong team," Jeff says and fake cries.

"You mean Matt's gay?" Sarah asks.

"I wish. He's straight as a pin. Too bad for me. But he is great to look at even if there's no hope for me. He is such a sweetheart. Jace threw me a birthday party a few months back because I turned thirty and I was so bummed about it. Jace threw the party at my favorite gay bar. Matt was a total hit. He danced with anyone that asked him for a dance. He even let me do a body shot off him. He was such a good sport. Ian was the lamest of the bunch. He sat in the corner booth and couldn't wait to leave. But Matt, oh, he was the man. He even gave me the perfect present, a Gucci messenger bag. I love it and take it everywhere. Jace did good too, Ali. He not only paid for the whole party, he gave me a two-week, all-expense-paid vacation on a gay cruise. I partied 'til I could party no more. You know what I mean? Those two. I love them like brothers. I have to say, you two have turned their world upside down, in a good way."

"I'm not with Matt, Jeff. I'm still engaged to Michael. We're just having a rough patch. But I would be lying if I said that I wasn't a bit happy that Matt stuck up for me. Thanks for stepping in so that neither one of them got hurt."

"No biggie. Now let's get your makeup on, doll face. You are going to look killer," Jeff says and starts to work on Sarah's make-up.

I start to dry my long hair, as it usually takes forever. When Jeff is finished with Sarah, she looks like a goddess. Michael should see what he is missing. Then Jeff starts to straighten the ends of my hair and pulls it back in a low bun at the nape of my neck to the left side. I love it off my face the way he is doing it. Plus I love that my hickey from Jace is showing. Jeff gets to my makeup and he is a master. I look great if I do say so myself.

Now it is time to play tug of war with my Spanx and try and lose my gut and thighs. I finally get them pulled up over my silk stockings with crystals running up the back seam. Then I put on my garter belt to hold the stockings up. I am going all out for tonight, for Jace. I put on the Japanese style bra that pushes your boobs together instead of just lifting them up. It is also a black silk. Then Jeff and Sarah help me squirm into my black dress. We have to position the dress just right so that the beige silk panels on the side show my tattoos and not the garter straps. The dress is strapless and my boobs look great. It is tight, but I feel good in it thanks to the Spanx. I look in the mirror and truly feel beautiful. I want to look this way for Jace. I want him to be proud of me tonight. Of course I hope he doesn't expect me to dress like this all the time. I can barely breathe after all, and forget trying to eat. Good thing I had a huge breakfast.

Jeff goes ahead to make sure the guys are ready and waiting by the stairs so that we can make our grand reveal to them.

"Promise to kiss me at midnight?" Sarah asks again as we put lipsticks in our bags.

"I kiss you, then Jace. Deal?" I ask her.

"You can kiss him first, I'll wait," Sarah says and laughs.

"Let's show them my work, glamour girls," Jeff shouts from the main floor.

I let Sarah go first and I can hear the whistles and catcalls the guys are giving her. All the guys are there. I feel stupid and nervous. I have to walk down the stairs so we won't be late, but now I feel too dressed up and too stupid. But I take a deep breath without breaking the dress and head for the stairs. When Jace sees me, he actually blinks his eyes a few times as if to wake himself from a dream. The guys all stare but say nothing.

"Okay, I'm going to change," I say and turn around to go back up the stairs when they all start to scream for me to stop.

"Baby, we're all just speechless. You look so, so amazing. So fucking rocker hot."

"Damn, girl, you clean up nice," Miles screams and whistles.

There are more words of encouragement and whistles as I get to the bottom steps. I slip on my not-too-crazy whore heels and tell Jace I am ready. He says that he has to get something from our room first and then he will be ready to go. When he is back a few seconds later, he looks high on love. For the first time, I see what everyone has been saying. I see the love he has for me in his eyes. They sparkle and shine like stars. I am lucky, and this is going to be the best New Year's Eve ever.

CHAPTER
TWELVE

Jace

I have Ali's ring in my pocket. When I get to the bottom of the stairs, I do a stealthy handoff to Jeff who hides it in his pocket. I am going on stage with a pair of skinny jeans and boots. There is no hiding a ring on me.

Jeff knows the plan. Once the ball drops, I'll drop down on my knee and pop the question to Ali. Jeff is going to slip the ring in my back pocket a few minutes prior. Matt has a part too. He is going to keep Sarah busy so she doesn't see the ring box and tip off Ali. Not that I think she'll ruin the surprise, but she might be a bit dumbfounded and give it away.

We are riding in a party bus to the event. Champagne and beer are already flowing freely. I am the only who really has to stay sober. The guys have played drunk plenty of times without missing a beat. But once I had too much to drink and slurred the words to every song and had people throwing things at me. Not fun. So I just watch everyone else drink and enjoy my Red Bull. I don't even need it to get all hyped up. I am so amped to be singing *My Light* to Ali and ask her to be my wife. I am even starting to feel confident that she is just going to outright say yes.

When we get to the venue we all go into the green room. The spread set out for us is pretty impressive. There are great looking hors d'oeuvres, fruit and cheese with crackers and plenty of champagne and beer. All of our assistants always made sure our favorite bites and drinks were in our green rooms before shows. This is one of their better jobs. I bet it was Jeff. He knows tonight is special, and looking at all that is in the room I can see he is helping make sure that Ali has the best night of her life. I am lucky to have him. After Ali says yes and I can take some time off, maybe Jeff deserves another trip?

Ali walks over to me and wraps her arm around my waist. "You okay, honey? You seem far away. You're not nervous about the show, are you? Matt said it's just a small set. Who else is performing?" she asks.

"Jeff, who else is here tonight?" I have to ask, since the only thing I am worried about is our new song and Ali saying yes.

"Raging Dark is going on before you guys and then Jay is performing after you and doing the midnight count down," Jeff responds as he walks over and hands Ali champagne and me a bottle of water.

"Jeff, honey, I can't help but notice that Lucas keeps giving you little looks. Is he gay?" Ali asks.

"Yes, but come on. That boy is way hotter than me. Not to mention, I don't think Matt and Jace would like the idea," Jeff says and sadly walks away.

Ali is trying to couple everyone up like Noah's Ark. I can't blame her. I have seen how Matt has been looking at Sarah. I did tell him to look after her and keep her busy. But I know Matt like I know myself. He is totally into her. I only hope he doesn't get his heart kicked in. Michael is a total douche, so hopefully Sarah will see it in time and turn to Matt for comfort. After all, when Ali says yes, they'll be spending a ton of time together. Wow, where did Mr. Cocky come from? When Ali says yes? I am so pumped all of a sudden. I look at her – she will say yes, she loves me. Why wouldn't she say yes, right?

Raging Dark passes by our green room to say hello

and we introduce the girls to the band. They only stay a few minutes because they are set to go on stage. That means we'll soon be up.

"Guys, start getting ready," Jeff announces.

"I think it's best if Sarah and I get set at the side of the stage so you guys have some alone time to get ready. Now kiss me, and lie if you have to, but tell me you're singing just for me," Ali says – and leans into me so I can look down her dress – and kisses me lightly on the lips.

"I will be singing only to you, baby. That's no lie," I say, and instead of the chaste kiss she just gave me, I kiss her with my tongue and push my hard groin into her belly. I just want to drive home the fact that I love and want only her.

"Okay, okay, don't rub it in that you two have each other and we're all stag on New Year's Eve," Miles yells.

"Please, Miles. You're gonna wink at some chick in the crowd and have security bring her back here for you. You don't stay stag for a second when we do a show," Alex retorts.

"I don't want to know anymore. Jeff's gonna show us where to stay so we're out of the way and can still see you. I love you. Have a great show," Ali says and wipes the lipstick off my face. Ali, Jeff and Sarah all walk out of the green room and go to the side of the stage.

"I don't think you have anything to worry about, Jace. She loves you. It's obvious. Stop looking terrified," Matt says to me and slaps me on the back. Everyone starts to warm up and gets ready to go on stage.

Then we hear a knock on the door. I think it is someone to give us a time check, but no such luck for me. It's Allen. "You guys ready to rock?" he asks.

We collectively roll our eyes. Like he knows shit about rock and roll. He just knows how to make us money and annoy us all. He is the one who started all the trouble between Alex and Cece, and I have such a bad feeling about seeing him at the show. He doesn't always come to our shows. So why does he have to be at this one, when there is so much at stake?

"What are you doing here, Allen?" Miles asks.

"I have to make sure my favorite clients are all taken care of. How is the spread? Everything okay? Do you guys need anything?" Allen asks.

Like he is going to do anything anyway. Jeff and Lucas are the ones who made sure we were taken care of, and they had done a great job. I really just want Allen away from me before I have to go on stage.

"Yeah, can you get out while we warm up for the show?" Miles asks.

"I wanted to tell Jace I was sorry. I was drunk and said some things. I'm sorry," Allen says. "I have a little present for you. I'll bring it to you after your set, okay?"

"I don't want anything from you, man. Just tell Ali you were an ass and apologize to her. She's by stage left watching the show," I tell him and then turn around and go to the bathroom. I just don't want to talk to him anymore and need some quiet time to get my head straight for the show. A few minutes later, Matt is knocking on the door that the coast is clear and we have five minutes 'til we hit the stage. I get my nerves in check and join the guys. Alex is twirling a set of drum sticks between his fingers. Matt is playing an acoustic guitar, and Miles and Ian are arguing about something stupid. My band of brothers. This is our preshow ritual.

Jeff pops his head in the door. "Let's hit it," he says and we all get up to walk out to the stage wings. We put our ear buds in and as we walk I give a little prayer that I will remember all the words and kick ass at *My Light* for Ali. I see her at the side of the stage talking into Sarah's ear. She sees me and stops whatever she is saying and immediately locks her eyes to mine. She smiles and blows me a kiss. I do the same and that's when the lights black out and the stagehands escort us on stage. Once we are in place, Alex slaps his sticks together counting us off, and we begin.

We go from one song right into the next one without much of a break. After the second song, Matt comes over to my microphone and speaks to the crowd. They are totally pumped up, maybe because of the music, perhaps because they are all drunk, or maybe because it is New Year's Eve. Then he counts us into the third song. Again, after the third song, we go right into our fourth song without much of a break. Then we all stop. The spotlight is straight on me.

"Thank you so much, LA! You've been great tonight. Happy New Year's Fucking Eve!" The crowd goes wild with screams and cheers. "We're going to play a new song for you now. You'll be the first ones to hear it, so pay attention. I wrote the words for someone very special and she's here tonight. Ali, this is for you. One, two, three, four."

I start to sing the first lines of the ballad and the band is right there with me. I try to look to the side of the stage to see Ali's reaction, but the lights are too bright and all I can see is light. I am upset that I can't see her, but I know she can hear me. When I finish the song, the crowd is going crazy. Alex leaves his drum kit, and Matt and Ian put down their guitars and we all come to the front of the stage and throw different things at the audience. Picks and drumsticks go sailing. I wipe my face with a towel and send it into the audience. Then we are off the stage and head back to the side of the stage. But Ali isn't there. I figure she must have been moved to the green room. So I start to move there, but

Allen stops me.

"Guys, do you mind giving Ali and Jace a second in there? Jace, Ali wanted to wait for you in the green room, to be alone with you," Allen says.

The guys pat me on the back and all wish me luck and walk off to a different room. I open the door and the lights are low. I can barely see anything, and before I can get to the lights, two hands wrap around my eyes from behind me. Ali is kissing my neck. Who gives a shit about the lights? I turn and start to kiss her.

"Baby, I missed you," I say in between breathy kisses.

But something feels wrong. This doesn't feel the way Ali's lips feel. I start to pull away, but arms are holding me tightly. The lights fly on, and it isn't Ali I am wrapped around.

"Jace?" Ali's voice sounds far off and strangled.

There in my arms is Corin, smiling, and her lipstick is all smeared over her lips. I guess it must be all over me as well.

"Corin, get off me! Ali, please listen. This isn't what it looks like. I thought it was you."

"You said you missed her. How could you mean me? You had just been with me. I really am just a rebound for Corin. I'm out of here." Ali turns and runs off.

I try to run to her, but Corin stops me and holds on tight. "Jace, she's not good enough for you. Allen told me you've just been with her to get me back. I want you back too. Come on, Jace, we're so good together and you know it."

"Corin, I don't know what Allen told you, but I love Ali. Now get off me so I can go after her." I forcefully remove her arms from me.

"Jace, what the hell?" Jeff asks as he makes his way in the door. "Ali's running out crying. Did she really say no and run?"

"Jeff, which way did she go? Corin jumped on me and Ali caught her kissing me, and she ran. I didn't get to propose. She thinks I was cheating. Jeff, you have to help me find her," I beg and almost start to cry. "What if I can't get to her?"

"I'll go see if I can find her, Jace." Jeff runs out the door and screams for the guys to go to the green room now.

All the guys come running in. "What did she say?" Matt asks.

"Change of plans. Corin just jumped me as Ali came in and fucked everything. Ali didn't believe me and ran. Guys, I need help."

"Corin, what the fuck? You guys have been over for so long. Why'd you come back now?" Matt asks.

"How'd you even get back here?" Miles inquires.

"Allen called me. He told me Jace wanted me back and that I should surprise him. If I screwed something up, I didn't know. All I know is I did what Allen said you would want."

Just then Allen shows up in the room and is met by five sets of angry eyes.

"Allen, you have to the count of five to disappear. Seriously. What you did was so fucked up!" Matt screams.

"What I did? I saved you, man. You cannot marry that cow and I know you were going to propose tonight. Well, you might not thank me now, but you'll thank me later," Allen yells at Jace.

"I seriously don't even know what to say to you. You have no right to say shit about my personal life.

Your job is to help us work with the record company, not fuck up my whole life, you dick. Either get it through your head, or you're out!" I yell.

"Why are we even giving him another chance? He pulled this shit with me and Cece. Now he's fucked things up with you and Ali," Alex yells.

"Alex is right. This prick is never going to learn until he destroys us all," Miles adds.

"This isn't the time to hand Allen his ass," Matt says. "We have to get Jace to Ali and fast."

Just then Jeff comes running into the room. "Dude, she got in a cab with Sarah and I heard her tell the cabby to take them to LAX. I tried to stop her but she wouldn't stop and listen to me." Jeff is in a panic.

"Jace, man, we have to get you there," offers Matt. "Jeff, go get the bus and tell the driver we have to hit LAX. I'm thinking if we hurry, we might even get there before her."

"Yeah, but LAX has like nine terminals, how do we know which one to go to?" Miles asks.

"We'll all get on our phones as we drive there and see who actually has a flight going out to Vegas. Plus there are six of us; we can fan out," Matt responds.

"Make that seven. I'm in," says Lucas, Matt's assistant.

"Make that nine. Ella and I are here to help too," joins Raymond as he starts to walk us towards the back exit, where Jeff has the party bus waiting for us.

"Alright, let's go," I instruct the team. With that, we all race out the door towards the party bus. We board the bus and race to the airport.

CHAPTER
THIRTEEN

Ali

I am at the side of the stage, watching Jace be so alive. He is electrifying on that stage. I can't keep my eyes off him. I even think that he tries to catch my eye from time to time, but the lights have to be crazy bright for him. After their third song, I feel someone tap my shoulder. I turn, and to my unhappiness I see Allen standing there smiling at me and waving me over towards him.

I hold up a hand to Sarah to try and relate that I'll be right back. She must have understood because she shook her head at me. I walk closer to Allen and he leans in to talk to me.

"Ali, Jace had a message for you. He wants me to walk you back to the green room to meet up with him. He said he has something important to tell you. So just stay where you are until I get you okay?" Allen asks.

"What's so important that he couldn't tell me before the show?" I ask.

"I don't know. He just wanted me to take you to the green room when he's ready for you. So just stay put until I come to get you."

"Okay," I say and go back to my position next to the stage . When their fourth song ends, I am happy to hear Jace say they are doing one of their new songs. Then I am stunned when Jace says the song is for me and he looks at my side of the stage. Sarah bumps her hips into mine and hugs me. I'm so glad she's having a great time. Because I know I'm having the time of my life. The words to Jace's song are amazing. The song is about a man in the dark his whole life and accepting that his life is supposed to be dark. But then he meets the light, and now he can only live in her light and love her forever. The tears are coming down my face. The song is so beautiful, and to think that I could have helped inspire this song has me stunned to silence. At least I don't look like a wreck. Thankfully I have on waterproof mascara. That was Jeff's suggestion. I'll have to thank him later.

The boys are on the stage handing out drum sticks and picks to the screaming fans. How is it possible this amazing man loves me? Not just loves me, but wants to live with me. Maybe that is what Jace wants to talk about. Maybe he wants to make sure I really want to live here in Cali with him. But right before midnight? Why now? Even if that is what the conversation is about, I know my answer. Yes. I came to that realization when I said it was "our place" during the massage, that my mind and heart were finally on the same page. They both want Jace, and want him all the time. I would move in with him, as long as he would move in with me too. I can't leave my job mid-year. I wouldn't do that to the kids. Maybe the guys would like to record in Vegas. If not, he and I can work during the week and have the weekends. When the school year is over, I will move. I will miss Sarah so much. But we will be only an hour plane ride away. I have to be with Jace. My whole heart belongs to him and I can't deny my heart any longer.

The guys are finally getting off the stage. "Let's go see the guys," Sarah says.

"Would you mind staying with Jeff for a few minutes? Allen said that Jace needs to talk to me alone."

"Sure, no worries. Go be with your rock star. Jeff

and I will go get some drinks and wait for the 'all clear' to come back and join you."

Just then, Allen comes over to me and puts his hand on my lower back to walk me back to the green room. He walks me over to the door and tells me to go in whenever I want to. Then he runs away. What the hell is that all about?

I open the door and the lights are off, but I hear Jace's voice. "Baby, I've missed you," he says.

How could he miss me? He had just seen me. I turn on the lights and think I am going to throw up. There is Jace kissing another woman. She is tall and skinny and gorgeous. And her lipstick is all over both of their faces.

"Jace?" I yell.

"Corin, get off me! Ali, please listen. This isn't what it looks like. I thought it was you."

"You said you missed her. How could you mean me? You had just been with me. I really am just a rebound for Corin. I'm out of here," I say and run out the door.

I run back to the side of the stage. Jeff and Sarah are there talking and drinking more champagne. I grab Sarah and try to remember how we had gotten into the backstage area. I pull her the whole way. When we are finally outside I start to tell her what I saw. I am talking quickly and trying to catch my breath. I feel miserable and shattered. I am trying to breathe. I can't catch my breath. I start to feel dizzy and nauseous.

"Shit, you look green. Are you gonna throw up?" Sarah asked.

"No, I just can't breathe. Sarah, help me I can't breathe," I choke out and start to fall. Sarah catches me and flags down a cab outside the front of the club. I see my escape and can immediately speak. I hear Jeff calling my name, but I ignore him and keep getting myself and Sarah into the cab. I tell the cabbie to take us to LAX and slam the door shut.

"No, wait, 757 Glenville," Sarah says.

"What are you doing?" I yell at her.

"Ali, I don't have my license or any money or credit cards. All I have is a lip gloss and tissues. We have to go back to Jace's house and get our stuff. Even if you don't want to pack up, we at least need our purses. Now, can you please just breathe and calm down?"

"Okay, you're right. I just don't know what I'm gonna do. How could Jace do this?" I start to cry.

"Ali, are you one hundred percent sure he did do this to you? Are you sure about what you saw? Could it have been a mistake? I mean, why would Jace have Allen take you to the green room? Doesn't that seem weird to you? Why wouldn't he have Matt or even Jeff take you to see him? After what you told me he did at that party and how the guys carried Allen out, why would Jace make Allen take you to the green room? Listen, you know I'm totally on your side, but I want you to think and think hard before you go to the point of no return. Do you really think Jace would write a song about you, tell the whole audience it was about you, dedicate it to you, and then go kiss someone else? That doesn't make any sense. Is there any way that this ass Allen could have set the whole thing up, hoping you would see Jace with someone else and permanently run off? Because look, you're running away aren't you?" Sarah asks.

Now that I think about what she is saying, it does sound more plausible than Jace cheating on me. Jace had just asked me to move in with him. And he seemed so happy that I had slipped and said that his house was our house. So why would he do all this and then kiss someone else? Sarah is right; this doesn't make any sense.

I need to think. What scenario does make the most sense? Then I think about the look on Jace's face when he saw me. He looked confused and terrified. It was exactly the look that I would expect if he did in fact think he was kissing me. Plus, if he did want to be with Corin, why had he said it was a mistake?

But then again, where is he? If he thought I was leaving, and certainly Jeff told him he saw me get into a cab, why isn't he running after me? Then again, where would he look for me? I don't even have my phone. What if he had been trying to call me? What if by running away I lost him forever? After all, where was my trust? My thoughts are stopped when we pull up in front of Jace's gate. I lean out the car window and enter the gate code and the gates open. We drive to the front door. I open the door and race to my room to get enough cash to pay for the car ride. As I pay the driver, with a nice tip since it's New Year's Eve, he asks me if I am sure I don't want to head to the airport. I smile and say no, that I am home.

I walk back into the house and see Sarah looking at me. It is almost midnight. I walk into the kitchen and pull a bottle of champagne out of the fridge and pop it open. I take two huge water glasses from the kitchen cabinet and add champagne until the bottle is almost dry. Then I walk into the living room where Sarah is still standing and awaiting my moves, and I hand her a glass. We clink them together and start to guzzle the champagne. We sit down on the couches in the living room, as both of us have turned ourselves to be facing the front doors. We drink and drink without saying anything to each other. Sarah knows that I am just waiting for Jace to get home.

I'm confident that when I see his face, depending on his expression, I will know what to do and say. Until he is home, I just have to wait it out, and get fucked up. I can't tell you how long we are sitting there in silence. We are more than halfway finished with our champagne when one of the clocks strikes midnight. I laugh and then plant a huge kiss on Sarah's lips, just as the front door opens.

"Well, at least she didn't run away from you for another guy," jokes Miles.

Sarah and I turn to see Miles, Alex, Ian, Matt, Jeff, Lucas and Jace all standing in the entryway with their mouths hanging wide open. Sarah and I laugh at Miles' comment. At least I kissed my best friend for New Years. I knew that, even though I was prepared to have Jace with me on New Year's Eve, something would get messed up. It always did.

"I think we should leave these two alone," Sarah says. "Why don't we all walk over to Matt's place and get drunk?" She gives me one last hug and looks me in the eyes. "For once, follow your heart and trust it. Trust you're worth it," she says before walking out the door with the guys. The door shutting behind them all seems so loud. There is nothing else but silence. Neither one of us speaks. We just look at each other. I don't move off the couch, and Jace stands rooted in the front entryway.

"Are you going to say something?" I ask Jace as I set the remains of my champagne down on the coffee table.

He rushes to me and wraps me up in his arms and lifts me off the floor. "Baby, I thought I lost you. Please, please don't ever run away from me again. If you would have just waited, Corin explained everything. Allen…"

"Set the whole thing up," I finish.

"How did you know?" Jace asks.

"When I calmed down and was riding here with Sarah, we started to think over what really happened and then the two of us thought it was strange that you would want him to walk me to meet you since you were mad at him from Matt's party. That's when Sarah suggested that Allen had set the whole thing up and it all made more sense. You're face when I turned the lights on, the fact that no one else could come and he had to be the one to walk me, it all seemed wrong and off. So, forget my suspicions. Tell me what happened," I say and start to sit down again on the couch, as Jace joins me.

"Just like you guessed. Allen called Corin and told her that I wanted to get back with her and she was to wait in the green room until I got there and she was supposed to kiss me. He set the whole thing up so you would walk in and find us. Corin wanted to let you know she's sorry. Allen didn't tell her about you and she's been out of the country so she didn't know about you. I swear on everything I have, I thought it was you. But when I kissed her, I knew it felt wrong. I was just about to pull away – in fact I was trying to pull away – but she had me locked to her. Then you said my name, so I knew I couldn't be kissing you and I pulled away. When the lights came on, and I realized what happened, I think my heart actually froze. I couldn't breathe when I saw the look on your face. I would never intentionally hurt you, baby. Please tell me you believe me, and that you know how much I love you, and that you know I would never hurt you. Please," Jace is begging.

"I know. I do now. When I thought about going back to Vegas, I felt like my heart was ripping out. Then I thought about everything we had these past few days alone, and I knew it had to be a mistake. You asked me to move in with you, so why would you cheat? I know I may be insecure, but I know you love me. I'm not sure why I am so lucky as to have you love me, but I'll take it. I take you. And the answer to your question is a definite yes."

"You mean you know?" Jace asks.

"Know what? You asked me to move in with you, and I'm saying yes. I thought about it and I know that I want to be here with you. I want this to be our home, our beginning. Why do you look so freaked out? What were you talking about?" I ask, very confused.

"I meant this," Jace responds as he starts to drop to one knee in front of me. Then he reaches into the front pocket of his skinny jeans, and pulls out a huge diamond ring. "I love you, Ali. I know we haven't had a traditional relationship with my being who I am and your being the most amazing woman in the world. I want you. Not just in my bed. Not just being my roommate. I want it all. I want you to be my wife. I want us to be a team. I want forever with you. Will you marry me?"

"Are you serious?" I ask, stunned.

"I was going to ask you at the first strike of midnight, so you'd have a happy memory for New Year's. But I fucked that up. I love you, Ali. I think I started to fall in love with you that first night we met. You love me for me, not my money or what I do. I love you for you. Please, marry me," Jace asks again,

"Yes, I'll marry you," I say through tears. Jace slides the ring onto my ring finger and then kisses it. I am back in Jace's arms. We are both crying, happy tears.

"You sure?" Jace asks.

"If you didn't want me to say yes, why did you ask?" I laugh.

"Of course I wanted you to say yes. I just thought I'd have to do some convincing. That's all. Oh, baby, I promise I'm going to be the best husband for you. I love you so much." Jace catches my lips in his and kisses me. I start to melt into his arms.

When I feel like my lips can't take any more kissing, I pull back and look into Jace's eyes. "You know, Jace, sometimes I can't believe that this is all real. I sometimes feel like I have to pinch myself to make sure

I'm not dreaming. I don't know what I've done to deserve you, but I love you and I am going to make you so happy as your wife. I promise. And thank you for making this the best New Year's ever. I definitely will never forget it, no matter how long I live."

"Do you like your ring?" Jace asks. "If you don't, we can always go back to the jeweler and change it. You can pick something bigger or a colored stone, whatever you want, baby."

I finally really look down at the ring. It is a huge diamond surrounded with smaller stones in a square shape. I have never been the kind of girl who thought she would get married. So I hadn't thought about what kind of ring I really wanted. This ring, the one that Jace picked out just for me, is the ring I want. And it is perfect.

"That's how I feel about finding you. I feel like it's a dream. I love you." Jace walks over to the stereo and puts on *Everything* by Michael Bublé. He walks over to me. "May I dance with my fiancée?" he asks holding his hand out to me.

"I would love to dance with my fiancé. Thank you," I say and take his hand. He holds me tightly in his arms, like I might float away like a balloon. It feels so right. I feel loved, and for the first time I feel beautiful and that this is all going to work out. We hold each other and dance a few more songs. "Let's go up stairs to our bedroom," I say and take his hand to lead the way.

As I start to take off my clothes, Jace walks over to me. "I just want to hold you tonight. You have no idea what it felt like when I thought I lost you. I just need to hold you, to know you're not going to run and that you'll still be here in the morning." Then Jace gives me a single sweet kiss.

I finish undressing and so does he. I want to wash the mascara off my face and try to forget all the crying, the unhappy crying, that I had done tonight. I take off my makeup. Then as I brush my teeth, Jace joins me and brushes his teeth too, next to me. I slather on some face cream, which I hope will ease the puffiness near my eyes. Then I go to Jace's drawers and take out one of his t-shirts and put on a normal pair of panties. I had taken off the thong, Spanx, and garters. Although I would love to start out the New Year with mind-blowing sex, I want to just be comfy and be held by Jace more. Jace has on a pair of boxer briefs and is already in bed waiting for me. He has a bottle of water and some aspirin waiting on my nightstand for me. I take the aspirin and then slide into bed next to him. We wrap ourselves around each other and fell asleep.

CHAPTER
FOURTEEN

Jace

I sleep well as long as Ali is in my arms. But at one point in the night, she is out of my arms, and I wake up gasping for breath. Then I see that Ali is next to me. I scoop her back into my arms and hold her. She's so tired she doesn't even move. Between all the champagne she drank and the scare she had thinking I was cheating, I think her body just needs to sleep. I hold her but can't get back to sleep. I just let my thoughts drift to her and the future. I love this house, but I also love her Vegas place. Maybe we could make it work, going back and forth between the two. I am willing to have the wedding anywhere she wants. I am going to hand her my credit card and let her have some real girl fun planning this thing. The only stipulation I have is I only want family and close friends there. I don't want a circus for a wedding. Then again, if that is really what Ali wants, she can have it. But knowing her, she will want the same thing as me.

I think of Ali walking down the aisle towards me in a fluffy white dress, and tears of joy start to sting my eyes. It is the most amazing image. My heart physically hurts and swells.

"What are you thinking about? Not regretting your proposal are you?" Ali asks in a sleepy voice.

"Never," I say and kiss her forehead. "I was just imagining you in a wedding gown, walking down the aisle towards me. You looked hot," I say and giggle.

"I'm hungry. I barely ate last night. Want to call the gang and we can have a huge breakfast party here and announce our engagement?" Ali asks.

"I usually host the gang on New Year's day with a huge brunch. Let's make a little something until Gino's crew gets here. Do you want to call the guys to come over for cinnamon rolls and coffee?" I ask her.

She shakes her head yes. I know she wants to show her ring to Sarah and tell her about my proposal.

There is a part of me that also is dying to tell the guys that Ali said yes without needing convincing. They had fallen in love with her too. They all proved that last night. They were all Googling on their phones and running around LAX like madmen, not one of them complaining. Jeff is probably going to enjoy wedding planning with Ali. Matt is going to love being in all the wedding shit with Sarah. The other guys are all going to try and screw the other bridesmaids. This is going to be awesome. I never really cared about the money I make. But now I am happy about it. I am going to be able to give Ali whatever kind of fantasy wedding she wants. The ring I gave her didn't cost too much. I just fell in love with it when I saw it and knew it would be perfect for her. It didn't even dent my bank account. It isn't as huge as I would have liked but I know Ali wouldn't have wanted something that big. But for Ali's actual wedding band, I already know I want a diamond band that goes all the way around her finger. After all, I am a rock star. She'll have to get used to some bling.

Ali gets dressed in a tank and yoga pants. I put on a pair of sweats and a t-shirt. We go down to the kitchen and start the cinnamon rolls. Ali tries to call Sarah's cell, but it goes straight to voice mail. So I call Jeff. Hopefully he stayed; he had a bit to drink last night. He picks up on the first ring.

"Well, boss, we're all on pins and needles here. What did she say?" Jeff asks.

"She said yes, and without any prodding. Now we would like to have you all over for cinnamon rolls and coffee before the huge brunch. So get all the guys and Sarah and get here pronto." I can hear cheers erupting in the background as Jeff tells everyone that Ali said yes. I am laughing. It makes me so pumped that they are happy for us. Jeff tells me that he'll ready the troops and they'll be right over.

I finish helping Ali with the coffee, mimosas, and cinnamon rolls. We are just putting everything on the table when the door opens and everyone starts to whistle and clap for us. They all look like hell, all except for Matt and Sarah. They look bright eyed and bushy tailed. What's with that? They look practically giddy. Maybe they are just happy for the two of us. After all, they are our best friends.

"Congratulations, my man. You did it. You have her forever," Matt says, as he man hugs me.

"Not forever yet, man. But soon enough. At least I'm on the road. And now, do you have something to tell me about last night?" I ask, eyeing Sarah who is with Ali, looking at her ring and hugging her.

"Not now. We'll talk later, but it's not what you're thinking, asshole," Matt says and walks over to hug Ali.

Each of the guys hugs me and then goes over to Ali. They all hug and welcome her to our crazy family. It is at that moment when I realize I have a true family. But someone, or rather, two people are missing. I go into the kitchen and call Gloria and Doug. I need them here fast. I don't tell them why, but let them know it is good news and that they are needed at my place sooner rather than later for brunch. I walk back to the dining room where everyone is taking cinnamon rolls and either grabbing a mimosa or asking Jeff to make a Bloody Mary.

Gloria and Doug arrive a few minutes later. After all, Matt and I had bought them a house just up the block from our homes. They know immediately that I had proposed. They say they heard the love and happiness in my voice. Everyone is talking and hugging and laughing. I loudly clink a glass and ask everyone to be seated at the dining room table. Everyone takes seats where they usually sit at my house, except Matt. Instead of sitting next to me as he often does, he sits right next to Sarah and has his parents across from them. Something is definitely going on. Good, I thought. Michael is a shit. I just hope Sarah is thinking the same thing.

I clink my glass again, and I stand there, waiting for everyone to settle down. Ali is seated next to me – another chair change, but perfect for me. I tell everyone to hold up a glass and that I have a toast to make.

"As you all now know, I have asked this wonderful and beautiful lady to be my wife. And she said yes. And I want to thank her. I want to thank her for loving me, for showing me who I am, and bringing me to the light. I also want to thank you all for helping me. Not just last night, when we were looking for Ali, but for always being by my side and having my back. Thank you for always taking care of me and for always holding me up when I couldn't do it myself. All the faces that I see now are my family and I love you all. I want to welcome Ali and Sarah to our family and tell them, you're in now, and there's no way out. Cheers."

We all clink glasses and drink. Ali kisses me before having her mimosa and we all start to eat the many cinnamon rolls Ali and I made for the crowd. The conversation around the table is light and airy. No heavy topics or talk of the incident of last night. That is until we all hear a little tweet and Sarah excuses herself to look at her phone.

"Fuck me gently with a chain saw!" Sarah yells as she jumps up and topples over her chair. All eyes turn to her and she is red with embarrassment.

"I'm so sorry. Please excuse my language." With that, she runs up to the guest room.

Matt goes to start after her, but Ali stops him and says she'll go see what happened. No one really spoke at first when the girls left the table. Then all eyes slowly turned to Matt. Even Doug and Gloria were looking at him.

"Why are you all looking at me? I had nothing to do with whatever is going on," Matt answers.

"Dude, don't jump on us, but where were the two of you last night?" Miles asks.

"I so don't want to hear this," says Gloria as she stands and goes in the direction of Ali and Sarah.

"We didn't do anything but talk. I think I might have talked her out of marrying that jackass. That was it. I told her how incredible I thought she was and how she could do better. Stuff like that. Then…."

That is when everyone's glasses freeze and all eyes are on Matt. We are waiting for the "then".

"Then what?" I ask.

"Then I kissed her," Matt answers and takes a big gulp of his Bloody Mary and looks at his cinnamon roll like it is the most amazing thing on the planet, clearly just trying to avoid eye contact with any of us.

"Dude, really?" Ian asks.

"Yes. And I'm not saying anything more. So just eat, assholes, and fuck off."

Gloria comes down the stairs then and grabs a mimosa. "It appears that Sarah's fiancé has put out a rather nasty thing about Sarah and you, son, on his facething account and said that unless Sarah crawls back to him today, he wants his ring back and never wants to see her ever again. But that's the nice version of events.

Jace, dear, we're going to need some more champagne right now to calm Sarah."

With that Matt rises so suddenly that he kicks over his chair and races up the stairs towards Sarah's room. The rest of the crew, of course, has to be nosy and soon are running up the stairs as well to watch and listen.

Matt and I get to the room to see that Sarah is crying on the bed with Ali next to her handing her tissues and trying to calm her down.

Matt advances to Sarah. "Let me see your phone, Sarah," he says, and she hands it right over to him. Matt looks at her Facebook account. Michael posted that he had caught Sarah on her knees giving Matt a blow job like a teenage groupie and that Michael left LA to go home and think about whether he would take her back. He wrote that unless she showed up at the gallery today and crawled to him on her knees, it was over and he never wanted to see her slutty cunt face ever again. As Matt finishes reading the posting, he takes the phone and slams it against the wall, breaking it to pieces.

"I'll buy you a better phone. Ali, everyone else, please let me talk to Sarah alone."

Ali looks at Sarah who shakes her head that it is okay, and we all leave.

Matt

I am going to kill that piece of shit. He posted on his account, knowing that Sarah's friends and family are all on his account as friends. He created a total lie and posted it to her fucking family. I know that is what has Sarah so upset. She could care less about what he said directly to her, but to say something like that about her, and have her family and colleagues see it, that was low, even for a shit like him.

"I'll kill him, Sarah. I'll fucking kill him," I say as I'm kneeling next to the bed where she is.

She gives a little laugh. "I know you're upset, but please don't kill him."

"Sarah, I'm going to fix all of this, I promise. I will make sure everyone knows that what Michael said was just a lie. I promise. Please, just please stop crying. I hate to see you crying."

"It seems that's all I'm ever doing around you. Thank you for being there for me. Why are you so good to me, Matt?" Sarah honestly asks.

"You're worth it, and so much more. I think because of Michael you've forgotten that. You're not thinking for one second of going back today, are you?"

"Are you serious? I told you last night that it was over. I can't be with someone who's just going to keep putting me down. That's so not me. And for him to write lies about me and drag you into it, that's just so horrible and immature. My parents and my brother are going to see what he posted. How do I bounce back from that? I'm sorry. I hope this doesn't put you in a bad position. I mean, I don't know if you're dating anyone, or if this will fuck you up with the fans somehow."

"Please, don't even think about me. I'm totally single and as far as my reputation, even if people thought it was true, who cares? Look at you. You're amazing. But let's not go there now. Tell me how to help, what to do."

"Just be you. I know Ali and Jace are going to tell me to stay here, but would it be alright if I stayed with you instead? I want them to have their time together after what happened last night."

"Of course you can stay with me. My place is all

yours. What else can I do?"

Sarah looks deep in thought for a few moments. Then she shyly looks at me, as if she is about to ask me for the moon. "Well, Ali and Jace are taking one of Ali's students to Disney tomorrow. He has cancer and Jace has arranged for a whole VIP day for him and they asked me to come. Will you come with me? I don't want to be a third wheel and I'll feel better if you're there."

"I love Disney! That's easy. Ask for anything and it's yours."

"Thank you, Matt. I think I just want to sleep for a while. Can you tell everyone?"

"Sure." I kiss her forehead and leave the room, closing the door behind me.

Everyone is waiting by the stairs. I tell them that she is going to be staying with me and that earns me a few smiles, and that she is going to sleep for a while. We all go back downstairs and finish eating.

Jace

We are all in the viewing room watching a horror movie when Sarah walks in and finds us. Ali is cuddled into my side, hiding from Michael Meyers. The guys barely notice her coming in, but somehow Matt already has radar on Sarah and gets up and sits in the back row with her. They are whispering and acting like they are the only two there. Very much like Ali and I. I know Matt as well as myself. I know he is head over heels for Sarah and if you look at Sarah, she is getting there quickly. I only hope it isn't a rebound relationship. Matt couldn't take it.

When the movie is over, Gino's crew shows up and

starts to set up the New Year's Brunch. There is everything – pastas, filet mignon, lobster, vegetables and different types of salads. I love going overboard every New Year. I feel like it is a way to usher in the New Year with good fortune. Sarah seems to be fine once we are all seated around the table. Gloria keeps talking to Ali and Sarah about different movies and books, trying to keep away from the whole wedding talk. After all, if what Matt said was true, Sarah is going to be ending her engagement.

I can see that Ali is so happy that Gloria is keeping Sarah busy, and that she is welcoming Sarah into this crazy kind of family. Ali keeps giving Gloria winks and smiles. Gloria keeps winking back when Sarah isn't looking.

Ali tells everyone that we will be hitting Disneyland tomorrow with Clark, her sick student, and his family. She invites everyone, but everyone except for Sarah and Matt declines. They all love Disney, but are scared that with all of them around, it might be too much for Clark and the security team. As it is, we are taking Ella and Raymond, and Ali even invited them to bring their kids along too.

Gloria and Doug say that they will come and meet up with us for dinner, but that is all. Everyone finishes eating and we are all vegging out at the table talking about this and that.

"So, what now? We recording in LA or Vegas?" Miles asks me.

"That's up to you guys," Ali answers. "I'm not getting in the way of the band. I have to finish out the year at my school, then I'll figure stuff out. But you guys need to keep doing what you've been doing."

"There are a few cool recording studios we could use in Vegas, as long as Ali doesn't mind us in her town," Ian says and smiles. He had resisted Ali the most but now seems to be her biggest champion.

"I'm down with recording in Vegas," Matt answers and then looks at Sarah.

"If everyone's okay with it, I think we should record there," I say. "I guess we'll have to check with, oh, fuck, we'll have to check with Allen and the label." I start to rub my hands over my eyes. How am I going to work with Allen? How am I going to talk to him calmly and not kill him? He could have ruined my life. He could have made me lose Ali.

"No worries there. We fired Allen last night," Matt responds and continues to eat as if it were no big deal.

"What?" I ask, dumbfounded.

"Yup," chimes in Sarah. "Your boys really had your back big time last night. Allen showed up at Matt's and was trying to say he was doing it all for the band and that they should kick you out because you were going to ruin their image, blah blah blah."

"This is the kind of stuff I've been worried about, Jace," Ali says with watered eyes. "I am not going to do this. I can't make you guys choose between him and me, and I'm not going to let you guys kick him out over me. We can still be together; we just won't let anyone know about us. I can just stay home when you do shows and I don't really like going out too much anyway." I can tell she is very upset and only saying those things for me. I know she would go through with it if I asked her to stay on the down low. But that isn't going to fucking happen. I love her and want the world to know it.

"That won't be necessary. We fired Allen. We can get a new agent in a heartbeat. You don't have to choose, Jace," Alex says. Then Alex walks away from the table. I can see the hurt in his eyes. Maybe we all should have banded together better to stand behind him when he and Cece were having this same problem. Now I feel like a shit. I get up and walk out to the pool, where Alex is.

"Man, Alex, I'm really sorry. I guess this really sucks for you. The whole Ali and me thing, firing Allen. I wish I could go back in time and not be such a self-centered dick when you were with Cece. I listened to Allen when he said you'd screw up the band with marrying Cece. I really liked her. I hope you can forgive me, man," I say and hold my hand out to shake his hand.

"No worries, man. We were all too young and stupid then. Maybe one day I'll find her again and maybe if not her, someone that makes me as happy as Ali makes you. I loved Cece and I know she loved me, but I guess just not enough. She was never really down with the groupies and the show schedule. I don't think my life was a fit for her. I'm glad to see that Ali fits in with your life, and with all of us. We all really love her, dude. Just don't fuck it up. Because as it sits right now, we'd all take her side instead of yours, man." He shakes my hand and then we are in a bro hug.

"So, what's going on with Matt and Sarah. What happened last night?" I ask Alex.

"No clue, man. All I know is I walked into Matt's room this morning to wake him up to come over and he was in bed with her, clothed, but they were wrapped around each other, asleep. I hope he knows what he's doing there. She's still engaged," Alex says.

"I have a bad feeling this isn't going to go well," I say and head back to the house. Ali, Sarah and Gloria are all in the kitchen talking. Sarah looks seconds away from tears. And Gloria and Ali have their heads together in a diabolical debate.

I go over to Matt and motion him to follow me to the media room. He does so without much nudging.

"Alright, what happened? Spill," I say to Matt as I close the door.

"We just talked and fell asleep. There was a kiss. One very long, intense and majorly hot kiss. But that's it. Nothing else, not even wandering hands. But I'm getting in pretty deep, bro. Already. She's perfect. What the fuck do I do?"

"Let me see what I get from Ali. There seems to be a big powwow in the kitchen with them and your mom. That's promising. Don't you think? Could be hard though, man. This thing with the ass munch could be hard," I respond.

"Put in a good word for me with Ali, would ya?" Matt asks and looks totally lovesick.

Now not only do I have to worry about my own love life, but also Matt's? This is crazy. But enough for today. I have a wedding to worry about, an album to get together and a lot of love to give to my girl.

I love everybody who is here in my house right now. But there is a part of me that wants them all to go the fuck home so I can have my woman beneath me, and on top of me, and in front of me, and in the shower.

I look over to her in the kitchen and she must have sensed my gaze. She is in the middle of talking with Sarah and Gloria when she just stops and turns to look at me. She winks at me and then turns back to Gloria and Sarah.

Gloria is now wrapping her arms around Sarah. She is hugging her and smiling at her. Then Gloria glances over to Matt and smiles at him and gives him a thumbs up. This is so weird. It looks like Sarah is talking Gloria about Matt and Gloria is loving it and helping Sarah out.

Their talk goes on about another half hour, then Gloria makes her way to Doug in the dining room and tells him it's time for them to go home. Gloria and Doug hug everyone and then they leave. Sarah and Ali go up to the guestroom to pack up Sarah's stuff. She tells us she wants to go and stay with Matt because she wants us to have some alone time, now that we are engaged. Ali and I insist that we want her to stay with us, but she is pretty adamant about going and staying with Matt. Then Ali looks at me and we both raise our eyes. Maybe this is a good thing for all of us, all the way around.

The guys are all going home, but they will see us before I take Ali and Sarah back to Vegas. When Ali and Sarah go up to pack, I pull Matt into the music room.

"Dude, I know this sounds stupid, but I don't think you should push shit with Sarah while she's staying with you. You don't want to do anything major with her, while she's wearing someone else's ring," I tell him.

"I know, man. I have been thinking the exact same thing. I want to be with her when she's mine, all mine. Is it cool if I tag along to Disney tomorrow with you guys? Sarah asked me to come be with her and I told her I would. I guess I should have asked you first if it was ok."

"You know you don't need an invite, ever. Of course it's alright. Listen, if you need us tonight, call us, or just use your key. Don't think that you'll be disturbing us, alright? We're here, especially if Sarah needs Ali," I say.

Matt smiles and shakes his head. Then the girls come into the room. "Hey, roomie, ready to head home?" Sarah asks Matt, and Matt puts a huge smile on his face at her words. Then he walks up to Sarah, takes her bag in hand and puts out his arm for her. She winds her arm through his and they head out the front to Matt's house.

Ali and I look at each other and then she takes hold of the outstretched hand I extend her. We walk up to our bedroom.

Ali

We are snuggled in bed after a very long and eventful night of sex. We have the house to ourselves. Sarah is staying in Matt's guestroom, or so she says. I know she is confused between her long ago love and newfound hate for Michael, and her new attraction to Matt. But right now, I only want to think about Jace and me . Tomorrow we have a day of fun planned. We are meeting Clark and his parents at their hotel. We will meet them for breakfast and then we will all ride together to the theme park.

I am happy that Sarah and Matt are coming along. I am hoping that someone will see them together and Instagram it. That would serve Michael right. Maybe I could help that happen. The thought of Sarah with Matt is making me smile. He is a great guy, and selfishly, it would be great for me to have her here, or on tour. But I just want her happy. I really know in my heart that Matt would treat her like gold and never make her feel badly about herself, the way that Michael has been doing. I am just very thankful that she isn't going back to Vegas without Jace and me.

When I talked with her and asked her if she would be heading back to Vegas immediately and trying to work on things with Michael, she told me that after a few nights of talking stuff out with Matt, she was pretty sure that the only time she would be seeing Michael was when she gave him back his engagement ring.

I must have had a smile on my face, because Jace wanted to know what was going on with my smile.

"I was talking to Sarah before she left with Matt, and she told me that she's going to head back with us, and give Michael back his ring."

"Why did you wait this long to tell me? I have to let Matt know." Jace is about to grab his cell phone and call Matt when I jump on top of him.

"No, you cannot tell him. Anyway, I think by now she's already told him. She wanted to tell him herself, honey. She wants to see if he wants to date her, once she gives the ring back. But I am supposed to keep this all a secret until she wants everyone to know. So play dumb tomorrow. That is unless they're all over each other and it's obvious."

"I'm surprised that you told me, if Sarah asked you not to." Jace is stroking my hair.

"I can't keep secrets from my fiancé, now can I?" I kiss Jace and then snuggle against him. "I don't know about you, but I need sleep. I love you, fiancé. Sleep sweet." I kiss Jace once more and hear him tell me he loves me, then he starts to sing The Light to me as I fall asleep.

CHAPTER
FIFTEEN

Ali

The party bus pulls up to Clark's hotel and we all go in to meet him and his family for breakfast. No one bothers us, basically because we have the table all the way in the back of the restaurant. When we are all done, we all get on the bus and head to Disneyland. Jace had put Clark and his parents up in one of the Disneyland properties, but we still need a way to get to the security detail that is waiting for us.

It is a blast. We have to have a small army of security guards with us at all times, but we don't have to wait on one line, to the unhappiness of the people stuck on the long-ass lines. We are doing all this for Clark, so I could care less. He is having a great time, always smiling and so are his parents. He loves the band Blacking Out, so having Jace and Matt there is a total bonus for Clark. Not to mention me. I was loving being out with my fiancé in public and not caring or worrying what Allen would say or do.

There are a few rides that Sarah and I just won't go on, so we send the guys and stay behind. I take a brief moment while the guys are all on Big Thunder Mountain to talk to Sarah about Matt.

"So, may I be so bold as to ask you if you stayed in Matt's room last night, or in the guestroom?"

"I stayed with Matt, but before you get too excited, we just slept. True, I did sleep wound around him, but we just snuggled."

"Sarah, I want you happy, with whoever makes you happy. But I think Matt really likes you and he is a really great guy. Did you tell him that you're giving Michael back his ring?" I ask her while drinking a huge cherry lemonade slushy.

"I did and as soon as the words were out of my mouth, before I could ask him to date me, he asks me if I would start seeing him more regularly once Michael and I were officially over. I felt terrible, because my reaction was that I laughed. I did that because I was going to ask him the same thing, but he beat me to it. He was so upset because he thought I was laughing at the fact that he asked me out. The poor thing. But I quickly explained everything to him, and now we're good. To be truthful, I tried to jump him, but he actually turned me down. He said he didn't want to do anything major with me until I was really his and only his. Isn't that the sweetest thing?" Sarah looks so starry eyed talking about Matt.

"Just be careful with him, Sarah. I think he's really into you, I mean, seriously into you already," I tell her.

"You don't have to go there, Ali. I know, you don't want me using him to get over Michael. The truth is, I haven't been feeling comfortable with Michael for quite some time. I don't know why I haven't told you, but I guess I felt embarrassed. Everyone was going on about my wedding at Thanksgiving, and I just really wanted to call the whole thing off. Don't worry, I'm moving speed bump slow with Matt and I just want to make him as happy as he's making me," Sarah says and is all smiles again since she is talking about Matt.

As soon as all the boys come back, I decide that we all need silly Mickey ears and go to get them. Everyone looks so cute in them. We continue walking but have to stop when we see Mickey Mouse – we simply must get a picture taken with him and with all of us in our Mickey ears.

Clark is having the best time. He is constantly on the rides with either Matt or Jace. Sarah and I are getting used to being each other's partner. You would think that Sarah and I are pregnant from all the different crap we are eating. We are even eating the giant turkey legs. Matt and Jace of course have to take pictures of us eating them.

The evening comes quickly and we are meeting Gloria and Doug for dinner at the restaurant that is set inside the Pirate's of the Caribbean ride. Gloria and Doug give Clark's parents big hugs as well as Clark. Then they come to all of us with hugs and kisses as well. Gloria seems to spend the most time with Sarah. I think Gloria knows what is happening with her and Matt.

Dinner is very nice. People are leaving us alone. At least it seems that way because the restaurant is pretty dark and no one can really see who is there. Clark isn't even the slightest bit tired, which is good. We want him to be able to stay awake for the fireworks. After dinner, Gloria and Doug decide to stay with us, and we all go start heading towards The Matterhorn. It is getting dark outside, so we ask security to thin out a bit since people can't really recognize Jace and Matt in the dark.

We are getting ready to board the ride when a girl literally throws me out of the way from boarding with Jace and jumps into the ride. The person who has the controls doesn't see, or doesn't care, and starts the ride while I am on the floor of the platform. Jace has no choice but to stay buckled up and remain on the ride. Raymond and Ella quickly pick me up. I turn to Ella and look at her with a stunned face.

"Did that really just happen to me?" I can't help but ask her.

"Sweetie, I would love to tell you that was the last time something like that will happen, but I like to be an honest person. It will happen again and again. We'll just have to make sure we have arms on you when you get pregnant so you and the baby stay safe," Ella says and then rubs the part of my arm where I had fallen and am scraped.

When the ride comes back, Jace looks ready to kill someone. He jumps from the ride and screams at the girl that she just hurt his fiancée and that it was totally uncool and that he was pissed. Then security is back and falling over themselves to apologize to Jace. Jace screams for them to kiss my ass and not his.

They all turn to me and start to apologize, but I'm not in the mood to listen and just tell them it's fine. I just want to go on another ride, whichever one Clark wants to go on.

Clark picks the Peter Pan ride and we are all escorted there. Clark loves it so much that we just stay on and go around the ride a few times. Then one of the security people tells us that if we go to Main Street, we can see the snow that is about to come down.

We make our way to Main Street and have security stay around us so we can be left alone while we wait for the snow to fall. The lights in the park dim and the song White Christmas starts to play through speakers around the park. Then the snow starts to fall from the trees. Clark is in his glory. We don't really get snow in Las Vegas. I think this is a first for Clark, and even though it is fake snow, he seems so happy. Seeing his joy makes me so thankful for Jace.

I am so happy that he set this whole thing up for Clark. But I know he did it really more for me than for Clark. I look over to Jace, who looks like a little kid at that moment. He looks enthralled at the snow and is singing along with the song. I wrap my arms around his neck and kiss him and tell him thank you against his lips. He smiles back against my lips and tells me he would always give me anything I wanted.

I know he is speaking the truth. Jace would do anything to make me happy. Just as I would do anything for him. I look over to Sarah and Matt, and they are wrapped around each other and locked in a kiss. I grab my phone and take their photo. I then post it on Instagram. I know I'm a bitch. But after what Michael said about Sarah and Matt, I feel like I had to do something back to him. Then I send the picture to Sarah and Matt's phones with the quote, "Sarah Pallur and Matt Trevinson, officially off the market."

They both get the text at the same time and stop their kiss to check their phones. It is dark, but I can see their mutual smiles about the picture. They look over to me, as I try to look as innocent as possible. They both smile at me and then go back to kissing each other. Gloria comes over and puts her arm around me.

"I am so glad see him happy, Ali. Thank you for introducing them. I know they'll be very happy together." Then she kisses my hair and goes back to Doug and starts to kiss him under the snow.

When the snow is over, the lights stay dimmed and the fireworks begin. Clark is smiling from ear to ear. His parents are too and chose that moment to come over to Jace and me and thank us for all that we gave Clark and them today. I hope that Clark will make it through this fight he is fighting. I hope today will make him so happy that he will want to do whatever he has to in order to get better.

After the fireworks, Jace and Matt take Clark into the biggest gift shop and totally spoil him. By the time they are done, they have even bought him a suit case for all the crap they purchased so his parents would be able to get it all home. They bought him shirts, pajamas, socks, a jacket, stuffed animals, pencils, pens, glasses, movies, and anything else that was for sale. Clark looks so happy as they all walk out of the store. But his parents just look shocked. I tell them that Matt and Jace really like to go overboard, and ask them not to get too upset. I think they are just in shock, and not really mad.

The guys load everything onto the bus and we head to Clark's hotel. Jace and Matt get off the bus and carry everything up to Clark's room for his parents and we all say good-bye. Clark's mom tells me that if all goes well, Clark will be back to school in a few weeks. I tell her I am going to be counting the days. I notice that when Jace and Matt come back down, Clark's father is walking them back to the bus. Jace hands Clark's dad a card and tells him that if they ever need anything, anything at all, to just call Jeff, his assistant. Then Jace hugs Clark's dad and gets onto the bus.

Jace and I get dropped off and Matt and Sarah come off with us too. They are coming in for a drink. Jace thanks Raymond and tells him to take Ella home and that he will see Raymond tomorrow. Raymond has to fly with us to Vegas, and then he will come back to California.

We walk into Jace's house and go right to the kitchen to get a beer for the guys and wine for Sarah and me. We all sit at the table for a while, just silent. I think the emotion of the day has hit us. None of us has kids. But now we are all thinking of poor Clark and his parents.

"I can't imagine the hell that those people are going through. I hope Clark makes it," Matt says.

"Me too," says Jace.

"Let's all toast to Clark," I say as we all raise our drinks. "To Clark and his family. May he win the battle against cancer, and be able to dance at our wedding." We all clink glasses together and have a drink to Clark.

After our drink, we all say goodnight and Matt and Sarah go to Matt's place. We tell Sarah we will pick her up at eleven. She is going to pack at Matt's. I go up to our bedroom and start to pack, then stop myself. Jace is behind me and sees me stop.

"Baby, what's the matter?" Jace asks.

"Well, I really don't have to pack anything because I'm gonna live here too. I just have to pack up my make-up case."

"Don't even pack that up. We can go shopping this week. I'm gonna need stuff to keep at your place. So I was going to go shopping with you anyway. After all, you did give me some drawers too you know." Jace comes over and hugs me.

"I love you, honey. Thank you for everything. Not just the beautiful ring, and all this," I motion around the room at all the clothes, and make-up table. "Thank you for the brothers and for Gloria and Doug. For my song. For this life that I will always cherish now." I hug Jace and kiss him.

Jace

I look into Ali's eyes. I can tell what she is trying to say. Her depression is always going to be a part of her. But she is now far from the bad place. She is happy. I can see her eyes clear and beautiful. I'm not worried that I will lose her right now.

"I love you, baby. I want to make it my life's mission to make you happy everyday of our lives. But when the darkness comes, I'll be your light. Just make sure you let me in, okay?" I am rubbing her arms.

"I promise, honey. I love you. We're in this together." Ali kisses me and I take her to bed. She is sad about Clark, so we just hold each other.

The morning comes too quickly. We will still have a few days before Ali has to go back to school, but I am loving having Ali at my place. I don't want to leave. But we also have to get Sarah back to Vegas so she can deal with the whole Michael thing. I have grown fond of Sarah and want her to end things with Michael so she can get things started with Matt. I just hope that Michael walks away like a champ and not as an asshole who fights and claws to hold on to her.

I look over at Ali. She is still tangled with me and asleep. I don't want to wake her up but we have to get a move on if we're going to make the plane. I really want to charter a private plane to be able to avoid the usual airport craziness. But Ali and Sarah don't really love small planes.

I untangle myself from Ali without waking her. I slip to the kitchen and make her eggs, bacon, toast and even freshly squeezed juice and coffee. I put it all on a tray and walk back up to bed. She is still asleep on my pillow. I love this woman, and I am going to get to wake up to her like this every day for the rest of my life.

I kiss her cheek and wake her. She smiles as soon as my lips press her cheek. She slowly opens her eyes and sees me standing there, holding the breakfast tray. She smiles.

"What's all this? What did I do to deserve this?" Ali asks.

"You agreed to marry me and make me the happiest man in the world. I love you, baby." I lay the tray on the bed and gently get into the bed with her. We both dig in to our plates with gusto. I love that she loves to eat with me, and that she feels comfortable doing so.

After breakfast, we put the dishes in the kitchen. Then we get our stuff together, including a guitar for me to leave at Ali's. Raymond is on time, as always. He loads our things into the trunk and we drive to Matt's. Sarah is outside with Matt when we honk the car. It looks like he doesn't want her to leave.

"Jace, tell her that I should come along now with you guys and not wait until next week when the band shows up," Matt says to me, begging with his eyes for me to agree with him.

"So not getting in the middle of this, bro." I'm not having anyone pissed at me and I'm not taking a side right now.

"Matt, let her end this shit with Michael, and then come to Vegas. She needs to do this on her own. We'll be there to make sure she's okay. I promise. But you have to respect that she has to do this, the way she wants to do it. Okay?" Ali is ever the voice of reason.

"See, Matt. She gets it. Now I just need you to have a bit of patience. I am going back, giving Michael his ring back, and then we're free to be together. Okay? Just trust me. I meant everything I said to you last night. I know it may be hard for you to believe me after we've known each other such a short amount of time. But if you want this to work out with us, you have to trust me. I have to do this alone. Okay? I'll miss you," Sarah says and leans into Matt. "I'll call you when I land. Now kiss me, so I can go and not miss the plane. And go get your stuff ready for Vegas."

They kiss and then Matt helps Sarah into the back of the car with Ali and closes the door. "Take care of my girls until I can get there Jace. Okay?" Matt asks me, fist bumping me.

"You got it, man." I slap his back and we pull away.

The airport is a zoo with tons of paparazzi. I guess they somehow realized that Ali and I got engaged, and wanted the first pics of Ali's ring. I did make sure that she wore it at Disneyland. Someone must have Tweeted it and now everyone is clamoring to be the first one with the moneymaking shot.

I turn to Ali in the back seat. "Honey, this is going to be a bit nuts. Just stay close to Sarah, Raymond and me, and say nothing, okay?" I tell her, trying to look calm. I am so scared this will freak her out and make her see the crazy side of my life.

She just shakes her head, and both she and Sarah look like deer caught in headlights. Raymond brings the car to long-term parking. Then he gets out and takes the bags. We don't have more than a carry-on each. Then I get out and put Ali next to me, and then Raymond sandwiches Sarah to his side. "Sarah, you too, say nothing, and keep your head down," Raymond says to Sarah. She nods her head in understanding.

When we go up the elevator to the terminal, that's when all hell breaks loose. The cameras and flashes are everywhere. They are pulling and pushing and trying to get between Ali and me. She holds on tighter to me, and puts her head down and even hides her ring under the sleeve of her hoodie. Security finally comes to our rescue and we are surrounded and then helped through the security checkpoint. After security check, we are taken to the first class lounge and security stays with us to keep people away. I see Ali sitting there, bouncing her knees and looking scared.

I sit next to her and just hold her hand. Then I bring her hand to my lips. "I'm sorry about that, baby. Are you okay?" I ask her, trying to look into her eyes to read the truth.

"Is it always going to be like that? Because if so, I'm going to have to wear make-up more often." Then she just smiles, looks at me and starts laughing.

"You're alright with all that?" I ask, totally confused.

"Honey, I want all of you. The real you. If that's something you come along with, then so be it. I love you, baby. A few cameras and a shoving match can't keep me from you. I'm marrying you, honey. I'm not going anywhere." Then she puts her hands on both sides of my face, pulls me in closer to her, and kisses me. Not just a little kiss. Her tongue is licking my seemed lips and I open to her. She pushes her tongue in, and then starts to suck on my tongue. When I start to moan, I pull away.

"I think we should save this until we get home," I say, reluctantly pulling away from her lips.

She is smiling from ear to ear. "You said home. Not my home, or your home. Just home."

"It is our home, isn't it?" I tilt my head in question.

"Absolutely. I love you, Jace Ryan Wikks."

"I love you, Ali Danielli, or should I say, I love you, future Ali Wikks?" I ask her.

"I want everything you come with, even your name. I like the sound of that Ali Wikks. But you know what sounds even better? Mrs. Jace Wikks. It sounds more like I'm yours and you're mine." Ali is smiling.

"I'll love you forever, Ali. I promise."

"Good. 'Cause I'll love you forever, Jace."

THE END,
for now.